THE CENTRE HOLDS

By the same author

JESUS ISCARIOT
GRACELESS GO I
THE RECTOR
PLATINUM JAG

THE CENTRE HOLDS

a novel

Anthony Storey

CALDER & BOYARS : LONDON

First published in 1973
by Calder & Boyars Ltd
18 Brewer Street, London W1

The author wishes to acknowledge with gratitude the assistance given to him by the Arts Council of Great Britain.

ISBN 0 7145 0902 7 Casebound Edition

Printed in Great Britain by
Galliard (Printers) Limited, Great Yarmouth

THE CENTRE HOLDS

"What are you going to do?" Margaret asked, gesturing round the empty sitting room.

"Why do you want to know?" I asked.

She was pecking round our house, collecting ashtrays, vases, the wall-plaques from near the stairs, even our wedding photograph which I'd propped on the mantelpiece that morning while the kids were saying muted, painful goodbyes before going to school.

She stood, facing away: "Just because we're separating doesn't mean I've stopped worrying about you."

She turned to look earnestly into my face, trying to guess if I was going to withdraw, as she called it.

"Did they instal your video-phone?" I asked.

The removal men came into the room, looking at her, then at the chair I was sitting in. I got out of the chair, ignoring the embarrassments, and they picked it up.

"Yes thanks. I really like my new house. It's small . . ." She indicated our . . . my house with her eyes. ". . . this place is too big. I never really liked it."

"You chose it, Margaret."

"Don't keep saying that. I was still at the stage when I wanted to please you."

"You've grown up since then."

We were both standing in front of the fireplace. I added, "I'm glad."

The removal men came in and started to roll up the carpet. She told them to leave it.

"That's all then, missus?" She nodded, dismissing them.

She wanted to have one last look round. I followed her up the carpetless stairs. "Oh, Tony . . ." She led into our bedroom. Outside, the removal men were banging closed their van-doors. She straightened the bed, and went on: "I always thought we were different."

"Maybe that's why."

She snorted, tucking in the sheets and turning them back. "You're different. It's high time you came to your senses."

"You mean I come running back to you?"

"That's just it. You see it as some kind of defeat."

She was bending low over the bed now. Her thighs and bottom looked cool.

"You're still a good-looking girl." She stood up, smoothing her short skirt. Pleased. She said, "Just think, I'm free now. . . ."

"I hope you'll let me take you out."

"You'll have to join the queue." Her voice was warm, teasing, hurt. "And for a month I don't want to see you. At all. I'll send the kids down at weekends when you're here. No video-phoning either. I don't even want to see your face." She glanced to see if I was hurt, then looked round the empty bedroom. "The first thing you ought to think about is getting some second-hand furniture."

"If I stay here."

"What are your plans?"

I couldn't tell her. "Coffee?"

She shook her head. "Oh, Tony, is all this worth while? I just don't understand it. We love each other. . . ." She looked at the bed. We'd been lovers the previous night, like fresh lovers. ". . . and here we are. The worst thing that could've happened."

"It's good," I said, going to her and taking her in my arms. "We've both got a chance to grow into ourselves."

She responded briefly to my hug, then pushed herself away. "Stop that," her voice harsh, "it's you who needs to grow up.

I've grown all I want to. All this is wrong."

"We've worked through that before."

The doorbell rang. I went towards the bedroom door but she slammed it. She pointed fiercely at me: "*You're* going to listen. For the last time".

"Something you haven't said before?"

"No, you bloody fool. Always the same. We love each other. We've got nice kids. You're damaging them. You're damaging me . . . probably yourself, though you don't know it. Chasing after moonbeams. And for what?" She waited.

I sat on the bed. The doorbell rang again.

"Come on, Margaret, let's be caring."

"I hate being caring. I've been caring. Ever since I met you. Where's it got me?"

I stood up: "We've had good years, bloody good. We've got nice kids. . . ."

She cut in, "If anything goes wrong with those kids . . .".

"Nothing will go wrong as long as they don't have to choose between us."

"How can you be so sure? And if they're harmed, my boy. . . ."

She was building up: face white, stretched, eyes glaring, her gestures stiff. "You've got what you want . . . you're free . . . to have young girls . . . to dream as you call it . . . to waste your life. You've wasted mine."

"You're just getting angry and . . ."

She shouted, "Stop telling me what I'm doing. I know what I'm doing. I'm committing suicide for you."

"You don't have to."

"That's a lie. Liar." She came towards me, her hands like claws. Her short, strong fingers, sharp nails, pointing towards my face. I sat on the bed, leaned back and placed my feet gently in her stomach, safely keeping her away. She clawed deliberately at my legs, opening the old scratches, gouging new ones. Through her teeth, "I could kill you. Kill you."

I wasn't angry.

"I don't want to kill you," I said.

"Well get me out. GET ME OUT."

"Margaret, you are out."

She was dazed. She shook her head fractionally.

The doorbell rang again.

She sagged. I got up quickly, eased past her and out of our . . . my bedroom.

"You took your time," David said when I opened the door. He came in promptly and led me through the empty hall and into the breakfast room. "I've been on the move since half-past six this morning and you keep me standing on the step." He put his plastic shopping-bag on the table, next to two mugs, two plates, two of everything. He sat on one of the two chairs. He still hadn't noticed the house was ransacked. "Didn't you want me to come, then?"

"Look, David, I'm terribly sorry. It's good to see you."

He smiled, nodding, "Yeah, but why . . .?"

I cut in, "Margaret's upstairs. She's leaving me today."

He looked around for the first time. "Where's she going?"

"I've bought her a house. Just up the road."

"An' you're keeping this, like?"

David had never trusted me. As kids, we'd lived next door to each other, never really friends. As grown-ups, we'd kept in touch episodically. "For the time being," I answered.

He smiled, his eyes cold. "And I can live here?"

I nodded. "Coffee?"

"Tea, please. Bought her a house?" He called after me as I went into the kitchen, "You must have plenty of money then."

"She's teaching. I've cashed my superannuation. We've always saved."

"You mean, you've given up your job?"

"Yes."

"You've been sacked!"

"It's impossible to sack a headmaster unless he . . ."

"I know . . ." he said. You don't know, I thought. ". . . unless he has one of the little girls in his study."

I made the tea, calling out, "Not even that."

" 'Ow's Jill, then?"

I stopped stirring, very surprised that I'd told him about her. He went on, "When's she moving in here? We'll have a nice little nest. I'll find a young bird and . . ." I took his tea in. He glanced sharply at my face as I went into the hall and up to Margaret.

"David's arrived," I said.

She was still sitting on the bed. She looked around, then stood up. I wanted to put my arms around her but she tensed instantly and would have exploded if I'd touched her. She straightened the bed-cover and went to look out of the window.

"I didn't hear the van go."

"It's those electric engines," I explained.

As she went down the stairs, David came out of the breakfast room. He looked at her, then at me.

She crossed the hall and opened the door. She turned, looked back, her eyes wet. Then she stepped out, closing the door quietly. I was still on the stairs. I didn't see, I felt David draw back into the breakfast room. I ran after her. She was getting into her car. "You're not beaten," I said.

She closed the door after her, let down the window by pressing a button on the dashboard, and started the engine. I thought she wasn't going to answer. The light whine of the engine changed as she switched on the drive. As the car moved forward slowly, I stepped along with it.

"Of course not," she said dully. She drove into the road. As if they were someone else's I felt violent pains, stretching pains in my guts.

David had made more tea. He handed me a mug. "What are you going to do?"

"Lose four stones, at least," I said ruefully. I weighed a hundred and seven kilos in those days.

"You can do with it. So can I." He patted his little belly with complacent hands.

I led the way, out of habit, into the empty dining room. "Did she take the telly?" he asked sharply. I nodded. He went on, "I'm sorry your marriage has failed. Which is my room?"

"We'll have to get you a bed today."

He was immediately interested. "I want to talk to you about that." He was looking me straight in the eye. "I was 'oping you'd lend me a few quid. I can't promise to give it back, like, but . . ."

"I thought you took bets in the prison."

"I did. I left my mate the business. He needs it more than me."

"How much did you bring out?"

He frowned carefully. "Well, nothing, really. I need some clothes . . . an overcoat, two suits, some leather gloves, a couple of pairs of shoes."

"But you've got some shoes."

"I've had these for years. I'm ashamed of them."

"How much do you think you'll need?"

"Fifty?"

"To buy all that?"

"To open an account, like. More tea?"

I shook my head.

Jill video-phoned that evening. Her oval face was drawn. She looked perturbed. "You've resigned," she said. I nodded, facing straight into the camera. "But no-one told us. Not even the Students' Committee."

"It's nothing to do with you," I said slowly.

"Is Margaret there?"

"We separated. Today."

"What's happened to you? Why didn't you tell me! Oh dear, I don't know what to feel. Are you alright?"

I nodded. "Look what she's left."

I panned the camera around the empty hall, watching her expressions.

"I'm on her side," Jill said.

"If there are going to be sides, so am I," I said.

"How are the kids?"

"Humorous and upset, of course. Michael said he was relieved. Not many of the parents of his friends are living together."

David came into the hall and Jill saw him. I introduced them. Jill knew about David. David hadn't used a video-phone before and enjoyed playing with it. "Tony told me about you," he said to her eventually.

"I wish I knew what's going on," I heard her answer. David looked at me.

"So do I," I said.

David and I ate little and drank much that night. He kept looking curiously at me. He insisted on telling stories of prison life and how he'd stuck out against the prison officers, counsellors, psychologists and psychiatrists. "They kept wanting me to admit I was deprived as a kid," he said finally. "I think it upset them more than somewhat that I gave them a blank sheet. Every time they tried me out I gave them nothing. Not even my prison number."

I opened another bottle of wine.

He went on, giving me another curious look, "Now you're doing the same to me . . . won't tell me what's going on."

"I wish I knew."

His face stiffened, eyes watching for my weaknesses.

"Everybody wants to know." I said. . . .

He drank, cocked his head to one side, and approached from another direction:

"How much do headmasters earn these days?"

"Quite a lot. It was a big school. We always managed to save."

"An' you didn't even tell Jill what you were doing."

"It's not because I don't have confidence in her. It's just . . ."

"Come on, spit it out."

He had me on the wrong foot. "Let me say this . . ." I mouthed, "Like everybody else these days, I find life meaningless. I've always worked well. Even conscientiously. I haven't been a bad husband and father . . ."

He cut in, "And a good 'eadmaster for Jill."

"Why don't you try to understand . . . that's since Margaret and I decided to separate."

He waited. I resumed, "I've shown responsibility and thoughtfulness to most people for much of the time. Even when I've been unpleasant in any way, I've felt suitably sorry. But I've never believed in anything. Not even myself. Without knowing it, my life has been meaningless. I think I've been waiting, all my life, waiting for something."

I could see his reluctance to accept the truth of what I'd said.

"And now," he said, "you're keeping me waiting for it."

"Oh, I don't know what it is." We were sitting on the carpet in the empty sitting room. He stood up and came over to the bottle. He filled his glass, then mine.

"I see. You've given up everything but you don't know what for."

"What about you?" I asked.

"I know exactly what I'm going to do. In fact, if you'd 've found me a bird, I'd be doing it right now instead of listening to all this bloody nonsense."

"I'm not your pimp."

"Who said you were a pimp? Just one of the really nice girls in your sixth form. Jill's mate, if she's nice."

"You wouldn't like my choice."

"Choice? What's choice got to do with it?" he said wonderingly. "I'm full of fucking sex. All she'd have to be is remotely nice and lie down there with her legs open. I'd be straight in . . ."

"You'd make a welcome of indifference."

"Eh? Don't come all high-faluting with me. I've known you since we were nippers . . .I'm the one who came and saw you in that mental hospital. Remember?"

"I'm quoting from a poem. About a young man carbuncular who visits a woman and all he wants is . . . he doesn't care if she's indifferent."

"I liked poetry at school."

"It's called 'The Waste Land'. Margaret's taken even that."

He stopped listening. He was dreaming.

"I'd love to meet a nice quiet woman with a couple of kids," he said.

We spent the rest of the night drinking, or rather, David did. I dozed off a couple of times. He wouldn't go into my bed and I didn't seem to be able to make the effort to get up the stairs. We both fell asleep just before dawn. The sun woke me up.

I was washed and shaved by the time David came to his senses.

"Where you going?" he asked.

"I'm catching the Monorail to London, and then I might go to France."

"What am I supposed to do?"

"First, get a second-hand bed for yourself. And a job. The house is yours to live in for a bit."

"Before you go, are you goin' to lend me that money?"

I counted out twenty-seven pounds. "That's all I can afford."

"Why not thirty?"

"It's a magic number," I joked.

He took out a bundle of pound notes and began to fold the twenty-seven into it.

"You've got money," I objected.

"Not much. There's fifty here. About three pounds for every year I did. Do you want yours back?"

I held out my hand, uncertain. He put my money in it. He said, "That's magic, alright. Now you have it, now you don't."

"I thought you had none," I explained, feeling small.

"Maybe it's better I stand on me own feet."

"Nothing crooked here, David," I warned him.

He palmed down my anxious expression. "You've nothing to worry about."

"And no lodgers. I don't want to come back and find the house full of neglected women."

"How long will you be away?" he asked, hopefully.

"I wish I knew."

On the Monorail I watched a television film of the urban fighting in the United States. Tanks fired at shadows flitting between windows in derelict blocks of new flats. A flaming petrol-bomb curved down onto one of the tanks. Flames exploded everywhere. The camera—the announcer's flat voice droning on—focussed on the narrow aperture through which the tank-driver could be seen struggling frenetically to get out. He screamed heavily, writhing half-out of the tank. Shots and explosions. His body jerked, then it was still. Ammunition in the tank exploded. The tank blew itself to bits. On the roof from which the bomb had been lobbed, two men raised their hands in victorious gestures. Two almost simultaneous cracks from snipers' rifles. Both men crumpled, one throwing his hands to his head, the other lifeless. It was Memphis, the announcer's drone told us. The most recent city in the United States—'United', that's a laugh—to become a battle-field. I was crouching in my seat, wretchedness outside . . . wretchedness in.

Dorothy, one of my few friends, was waiting in the foyer of the BBC. I'd asked her to show me the film of an interview of someone I'd very slightly known years previously. I knew of the interview, which had never been shown publicly, and that it was very unusual. It had long been my intention to try to see it.

"You've put on weight," Dorothy said as we kissed.

"I'm taking it off now," I answered, stepping back to look at her. Before I'd married we had been lovers. She'd made a man of me, she used to say.

"You look tremendous," I said.

"For my age, you mean."

"You're how old? Forty-seven?"

"I never think about it. Still married?"

"We separated. Yesterday."

"I always said you'd be unable to sustain a real relationship. How's Margaret?"

"She's not too bad. She's worried about me. I gave up my job."

Dorothy didn't say anything for a moment, then: "What are you going to do?"

"Not work for a bit. If this film means anything I may go to France . . . follow it up."

"It means nothing to me. It's rather a bore."

I could understand Dorothy's reaction. It was an interview with a woman, Mary Johnson, who about twelve years previously had created minor disturbances in a village in Yorkshire by announcing she was carrying God's child. I was 'breaking up' at the time. My life was difficult. I'd kind of split away from what was going on around me. In the end I went into a mental hospital, and it was a psychiatrist there who had told me about Mary Johnson. He talked to me about many things, but what he told me about this woman made a mark. He was treating her fiancé, Christopher something-or-other. He'd been driven bloody crazy by her mad annunciation. Except that if he had been mad there would have been different problems. Her family apparently believed her, or at least had difficulty not-believing her. Christopher used to wander about the hospital murmuring things like 'C. . . c. . . cuckolded by g. . . g. . . god." None of the gods there took his accusations very seriously.

I understood that the psychiatrist had some reason for telling me about Christopher and Mary. Also, he took the trouble to make me read Mary's father's novels. He was one of the two or three writers who got people reading novels again. Mainly, so far as I could tell, by extending the novel into the common ground between theology, fiction and anthropology, not to mention psychology. I found his writing interesting but I cared little about all this until I met Mary Johnson. She was walking through the grounds. Eight months pregnant. She walked freely, wearing slight clothing. Her belly swayed beautifully. She was open. Taking in everything and giving everything out. I can't describe how she was. Her emanations were round, full and good. Nothing, not anything mad about her, or even strained. And yet she must've been bloody crazy. And yet again, seeing her I sensed my own sanity. I got a brief exposure to my own healthy self. We smiled. I walked with her. We said nothing. I knew I was a whole person in her experience, though not in my own. . . .

"I met Mary Johnson once," I told Dorothy.

"I know, you told me on the 'phone. She's frightfully stiff . . . arrogant in this film." Dorothy's voice was contemptuous, vicious.

The interview was short. And astounding. Mary, as when I'd met her, was radiantly pregnant. She wore very light clothing so that her body, when she moved, was easily seen. She held the child in her hands from time to time, as if in a touch-dialogue with him. Her interviewer, a rather nervous man called Bryan King, asked her routine questions to start with. She was quite relaxed and good to look at. As the interview went on, her answers seemed to make King uneasy. She was implying that the child she carried was very unusual. At one stage, Mary stood up, wanting to go to him. Her idea was, I suppose, to reassure him. But he told her, speaking coldly, to sit down.

KING *Tell us simply what you feel is special about the child, Miss Johnson, you're carrying?*

She turned fractionally, looking straight into the camera. She waited, as if listening to voices inside her. Her face was complete. Her fecund body was perfectly relaxed. She touched her child with both hands so that her arms made a circle.

MARY *I am carrying God's child, which will be a boy.*

She continued to look into the camera. Kind of underneath her cool exterior was a tender fierceness. Strength. Concern that her truth should be known.

KING *Am I getting it right? You're saying you're pregnant by God?*

MARY *Yes.*

King was stretched. I didn't believe her but it didn't make *me* nervous. In fact she made me feel at ease. There was nothing about her to suggest maladjustment, stupidity, disturbance. She appeared convincingly intelligent, and well-aware of the pitfalls of her incredible claim. She watched King, increasingly alert to his growing tensions.

KING *Is there any doubt about your condition?*

Mary shook her head.

MARY *You can see for yourself. The child moves in my womb.*

She looked at her abdomen.

MARY *About my mental condition, there are many doubters.*
KING *You must count me one of them, Miss Johnson. What you're asking me—and a huge audience—to believe is unbelievable.*
MARY *I know.*
KING *Frankly, your claim is blasphemous.*
MARY *That God is the father of my child distresses you.*
KING *That you tell me he is . . . that distresses me. It's blasphemy, among other things.*
MARY *What does God care about blasphemy? You make him small.*

King shifted jerkily on his seat. He glanced round the studio, unsure.

KING *But it's surely the easiest thing in the world to say you're expecting God's child?*
MARY *The hardest.*

King stared at her. He suddenly remembered he had papers in his hand. He shuffled them nervously, finding the one he wanted.

KING *You know, Miss Johnson, I sent my researchers round several mental hospitals and they tell me that there are women in each who make the same claim.*

MARY *It's a usual delusion, an attractive one, of mentally and emotionally ill women. And I think your researchers if they enquired would find that among ill men, divinities aren't all that rare. They make brave sense for one who wishes to understand. Can you put away your mockery and cynicisms, Mr King?*

Mary stood up again, going temporarily out of view. The camera shifted quickly to get her in focus as she walked over to King. King cowered away from her, putting his head in his hands.

This wasn't like watching television. I felt I was there. This awesome woman was attacking a run-of-the-mill interviewer with irony, goodness and pure intelligence. I looked at Dorothy who was staring at the screen, tears falling down her face.

Mary put her hands behind his neck and held him, eventually supporting his head when he looked up into her face.

MARY *Are you a Catholic?*

King nodded.

MARY *Can you not believe in miracles, Mr King?*
KING *Not really, Miss Johnson. Please go back to your seat.*

As she walked across the studio, a technician, bearded like Christ, appeared behind her, staring, his face contorted. Mary sat down and faced King.

MARY *What do you mean when you affirm in church that Jesus was born of the Virgin Mary?*

The Christ-technician got nearer, becoming increasingly agitated. Mary hadn't seen him.

KING *But that was two thousand years ago . . . it was a miracle.*

MARY *Miracles come out of the deepest imaginations of men. They're with us always.*

Mary suddenly saw the Christ-technician and stood up, her face open to him. He smacked her with force. She staggered, regained her balance, and faced him again, her hands holding the child in her belly. The Christ-technician groaned from deep in his chest. He stared at her, rage building up inside him. He swung at her, on his toes, all his weight behind his open hand. Mary was knocked off her feet.

A second man—her father I now know—burly, ferociously aggressive, appeared in the desperately swivelling cameras. He clubbed the Christ-technician to the ground and fell on him, driving powerful blows at his head.

Mary was lying on the floor. Her short dress crumpled up. Firm thighs, white pants and naked, swollen belly were exposed. Nobody interfered.

The technician weakly fended off the blows that were aimed with decreasing vigour.

Mary's head cleared.

MARY *Oh . . . Anthony . . .*

She got up unsteadily and stopped her father from further violence. She helped the bruised technician to his feet. Bryan King held his head in his hands. He looked up, his face blurred by tears. He stared at Mary who was helping the technician across the studio.

"Some interview," I said.

"Do you want to see it again?"

"Could I?"

Dorothy gave the necessary instructions to the operator in the control-box at the back of the viewing room.

"Don't be taken in by her." She was attempting to articulate with certainty. "I've heard that she had a girl. That's how much she knew about it. This friend of mine saw them in France and the child is a girl." Dorothy was speaking angrily now, almost to herself. "That son of God she was so certain about is a girl."

I don't remember clearly what happened for the rest of that day. Dorothy introduced me to a television producer, Alistair Shuttleworth, and two almost identical young women, Emma and Sybil. I remember not-eating lunch with them. We were in a warm, subdued restaurant. They were talking about sex. I recollect Dorothy saying that she no longer felt strongly whether it was a man or woman. "I'm not desperate or demanding . . . wanting orgasms . . ." She glanced at me, thinking more about my state of mind than my reaction to what she was saying. I didn't have a reaction. She continued, ". . . what matters to me are the feelings."

Alistair Shuttleworth—well-dressed, bulky, warm, explosive—put an arm round each of the two young women. Neither moved to accommodate his gesture. I felt they were all watching me.

Later Alistair asked what I thought of the Mary Johnson film.

"I don't know why you wanted to see it," Dorothy observed.

I looked at her. She went on, "Alright, I suppose I do know. But she's a terrible fraud, don't you think?"

Again I felt an alert interest in my reaction. As if Emma, Sybil and Alistair were depending in some way on what I felt. The awkwardness lasted for several minutes. We were all silent. Things were going on between us that none of us wished to verbalise.

I got home at two in the morning. There was a scruffy armchair in the sitting room. Half-awake, I fell into it. I kept seeing bits of the interview over and over again.

I dozed from time to time. I was very pleased to see, at dawn, the tree in the front garden. Birds—picking, perching, squabbling—occupied it splendidly. David must have heard me come in because he popped his head round the door, commenting on the fact that I'd said I was going to be away for some time. I was in a daze.

"As unreliable as ever," he added, looking at me quizzically. Then, "That's one thing I did learn in the nick. When a fellow wants to be on his tod."

The next day, the doorbell rang.

"Meet Bryan King," Alistair Shuttleworth said when I opened the door. Bryan was fat now, and looked settled. "That's sudden," I said as I led them into the sitting room. Alistair explained, "Dorothy mentioned you might be going to France. I wanted to catch you before you went. Too sudden?" I turned to Bryan King, "Alistair told you I saw that interview you did with . . ." "With that mad woman," Bryan cut in. He spoke cynically, but I couldn't feel whether his tone was directed at Mary or himself. I went and got a bottle of wine, two mugs and a glass.

"You think she's mad?" I asked.

"She was a dangerous simpleton . . . I don't mean she didn't have brains. But she'd absorbed her father's mythology so completely that she didn't know who she was."

"I saw it twice. You were crying . . ."

"Things were bad for me at the time. I'd abandoned Marxism, I was still struggling with Catholicism. She's dangerous. She triggered off something that's taken me years to get over."

"Have you got over it?"

"Immediately after that I lost my job . . . she cost me my job. I went to work in Poland. I'd still be there if the army hadn't gone on strike." He looked at me to see if I knew what he was talking about. "I was in Warsaw when the police fought the army. I got stuck in my flat and had to stay for nearly six weeks. I managed to get petrol for my car a couple of days before the Russians came in. Otherwise . . ."

I filled his glass. His evasion stood out a mile.

"Then I got back to England and Alistair offered me work with Yorkshire Television."

I noticed that Alistair was looking at me. He deferred to Bryan in case he wanted to say anything else, then asked: "Well, what did you think of her?"

"I believed in her," I said.

"Yes," said Bryan, "it all depends on your angle. She uses words that are still very powerful . . . 'god', 'holiness', 'miracle', like Father Corcoran at my school. But the way she uses them makes your own doubts about them, proper doubts, disappear." He emptied his glass. "You're left facing up to the most frightening aspects of your own fears."

I poured more drink in their glasses. I wasn't drinking.

"That," I said, "is if fears are all one's got. If one has hope of any kind . . . if one's basic nature is hopeful, then her effect might be to leave one facing up to the most frightening aspects of one's own hopes."

None of us spoke for a bit. I think Bryan was embarrassed. Then he said: "Anyway, I've left all that stuff behind me, way behind." He sounded almost confident. "I got married, had a couple of kids, got to know Poland pretty well. Now here I am. Waiting to take over Alistair's job if he decides to leave."

Alistair explained that he was dissatisfied with what he was doing and had been offered another job that he might take. He also told me that he was going to see Jane Johnson, Mary's mother, and if I wanted to meet her he would take me with him. She lived near Ilkley.

For the first time Jill actually slept with me that night. Her young body perched strangely on my bulk. I hadn't seen her completely naked before. She was slimmer than I'd imagined, her hips almost boyish, her breasts tiny and firm. I remember trying to persuade myself that sex added to her innocence. And mine.

I woke early in the morning, my guts in stretching physical pain. Head tense. I lay there, trying to be still. I had to bring my knees up to my chest to minimise the pain. Jill woke up.

"I'm being torn," I said.

She laughed. It *was* funny, I thought. I got out of bed and walked around the house. Bending and turning my trunk. I tried to avoid Jill, not wanting her to think that this was a cheap way of persuading her to make love again.

She made coffee. There were some of Margaret's sleeping capsules in the bathroom. I took half of one. Jill went back to bed after making sure there was nothing she could do. I read until my eyes blurred with the drug.

Alistair drove me to see the mother of Mary Johnson. When we were through Ilkley and near her village he pointed out the church, unused it seemed, where Mary Johnson's fiancé had been the rector. Alistair wanted to show it.

Before getting out of the car he said: "I think you ought to know that my interest in the Johnsons is at least partly professional. I'm playing about with the idea of getting involved in Religious Broadcasting. If I decide to do it, I would be radical."

"With Yorkshire Television?"

"UNESCO are building a trans-continental set-up."

"Using the existing networks?"

"They're building their own transmitters, everything."

I started to get out of the car.

"Guess where," he said.

For a moment I thought he meant where we were. I glanced around for evidence of building. Then I realised he meant in France.

"France?"

"Not just France. On the high plateau just outside Beauvais."

"Isn't that where Mary Johnson is living?"

We looked into each other's eyes. I said, "I'm becoming surrounded by meaningful coincidences."

He smiled.

"God!" I exclaimed.

"Yes?" he asked.

"Weak joke."

"Depends on who's joking." He got out of the car. "In fact, I've been asked to run the religious broadcasts. One of the things I need to think about is whether I can find the right kind of people to work with."

There was a quiet flash of light in my mind." Is that a problem?"

Again we looked at one another.

The church was very dusty. In the corners were rotting leaves from several years. The windows were veiled with heavy, grimy cobwebs. Alistair lead me to the famous east window which had been designed by Blake in 1804. Blake's sharp sense of line stood out. Alistair pointed out the Madonna seated with the divine child on her knee. Even through the muck I immediately sensed her profound fulfilment. I said, "She's so slim, and marvellously mysterious."

"Her bloody kid's got the face of an old man."

"Do you know that poem of Blake's about a baby boy being given to 'a woman old' who nails him to a rock and 'catches his screams in a cup of gold, and she grows young as he grows old'?"

Alistair shook his head, impatient to show the window opposite. It was entirely plain glass except for the top panel which was medieval, probably thirteenth century. Alistair climbed precariously onto the pulpit, balancing dangerously on the outer rim to point up at the panel. A fecund woman was formally represented with round strong shoulders and full thighs. Her breasts were golden-yellow, her body red. Inside the outline of her body was the outline of a church, the spire between her breasts.

"Look where the door to the church is," Alistair said, excited.

I saw it. "It's her sex."

He turned to me, his excitement mounting. He shouted, "Exactly!" He raised his arms, half-falling off the pulpit, landing awkwardly. We both began to laugh.

"Of course it's her sex," a woman's voice, not unlike Margaret's, called out.

A short, strongly-built woman, smartly dressed, stood under the Blake window. She smiled slightly.

"You're like two little boys caught playing with yourselves."

"In Church too," Alistair added. He introduced me as she stepped forward, firmly offering her hand:

"Jane Johnson," she said. I shook her hand—dry, strong, though slightly arthritic. She shook hands with Alistair.

"I didn't tell Tony that you'd invited us for lunch. I thought I'd surprise him."

"Perhaps he doesn't wish to have lunch with me."

Her insecurity was neither polite nor contrived.

"I'd love to have lunch," I answered, "so long as you don't mind if I don't eat much."

She looked at my bulk:

"You could do to lose a stone or two, I'm sorry, kilos," she said. "There now, bitchy and we've just met."

"It's more than just losing weight . . . it's a whole attitude somehow . . ."

Jane had roasted a duck. They ate with their fingers while I nibbled at the salad. I couldn't stop myself looking at the crisp, tasty skin. They both ate quickly. Alistair glanced several times at the carcass on the large serving-plate next to Jane. He seemed to know her well enough to reach across and seize the delicious fragments that remained. I wondered if they were lovers. Alistair said:

"One of the Edwardian poets wrote that if a man would be wise, he must begin at the knees of a woman . . . it shows how bloody primitive the Edwardians were compared with the guy who designed that window, in the thirteenth century."

Jane had a superb trifle waiting on the sideboard. She didn't offer me any, sensing, I think, that I would have accepted. She said to me:

"I understand you're interested in my daughter."

"In her ideas."

"They aren't her ideas. They're her father's."

"They aren't exactly his, either," I replied. She looked keenly at me. She said,

"I agree . . . I've never really thought of him as original . . . I know he's a good writer, but I think his ideas came from one of his tutors at Cambridge."

"Oh, I'm not suggesting he's not original."

"Don't mind me!" she said, eating her trifle quickly. "I'm a plain woman and if you want to get to know me you'll have to put up with it. I think he's vastly over-rated . . . and that's not jealousy talking."

"Come on now, Jane," Alistair protested, "jealousy comes into it somewhere."

She stopped to think, nodding, then swallowed another spoonful of trifle. My mouth watered. The cream was thick, stained with raspberries and myrtle.

"Doesn't he live in France?" I asked.

She said, looking at Alistair, "I am jealous, I suppose. He's always got what he wanted. I'm not saying he isn't very clever. It's just that I don't think of him as original . . . he's quick to pick up ideas. Mary gave him a lot of ideas . . ." I cut in:

"So Mary *has* ideas of her own."

"He's the cleverest man I've ever known. She's the cleverest person. No-one has a chance with her. She seems to know . . . well . . . everything."

"Is she still that much under your skin?" Alistair said provocatively.

"She remembers everything . . . she distorts it . . . she's devious, and if she doesn't know something she finds out efficiently."

Alistair was leading her. "You're speaking very coldly of your own daughter."

"I know it's an awful thing to say but I hate her." She repeated, whispering, "I hate her."

Jane was preoccupied with her thoughts, and spoke deliberately. She needed to talk and wasn't interested in whether we understood. "She's destroyed so much of me . . . of my life . . . of what I wanted . . . I know it's not her fault," she looked quickly from Alistair's face to mine, "but it's not my fault either."

Alistair began to speak but Jane cut in:

"I should never have had her."

Her words were mechanical. She had said them, or thought them, many times. Her choice of words, her tone, her stiff, angry gestures, even the way she flushed rapidly, reminded me again of Margaret. She got up and made her way to the garden, assuming we would go with her and listen.

"Everywhere I go nowadays they ask about her." She laughed, looking back as we followed. "She predicted that would happen . . . not that exactly, but she's always said all she has to do was concentrate on that child of hers and everything else would follow . . . every-*one* else would follow. She's mad. She's supposed to be so clever but how could someone with her brains think she's conceived God's child? If only she'd say who the father was . . . I wouldn't mind."

"A lot of people," Alistair said, "think your husband is the father."

"I used to think he was . . . I still think he wanted her. I know. They used to sit here talking to me . . . to *me* . . . his wife and her mother, about whether they should have each other . . ." She mimed her husband: " 'The only limits to our love are those imposed by my neuroticisms and inhibitions . . .' They're inseparable."

"That doesn't mean he wanted her," Alistair objected. I realised that they'd had this conversation a number of times.

"I know it doesn't, but do you think I'm lying? They talked with me about whether they should do it . . . and he was always chasing girls. Again, I was supposed to understand . . . he kept telling me I had to understand. Well, I understand now he has to struggle to . . ."

She stopped, somehow relieved. She looked at me:

"Well, I suppose you're shocked. All the world seems to be going over to their side . . ."

"I'll go and make some coffee." Alistair got up. Jane assented, vaguely waving her hand towards the kitchen, indicating he knew where everything was. She stood up, and started to wander about the garden. I could see her breasts were still firm and except for bulges round her waist and at the top of her legs—her dress was opaque against the sun—so was her body. She looked at me suddenly.

"Do you think they could be mad?"

She was almost consciously offering me a prize if I gave the right answer.

"You're an attractive woman," I said.

"For my age, you mean."

"No, I mean attractive."

"Are you married? You must be."

I nodded.

"Do you live together?"

"We separated, caringly, about two weeks ago."

"God," she said condescendingly, "the way you say that. You and my husband have a lot in common."

She strolled around, then:

"I suppose you like young girls as well."

I felt exposed, silly. She looked at my face and shook her head. She said:

"Well, don't look so ashamed."

I remember saying, "I like sex so long as it's not possessive."

She listened to what I said and thought about it. I suddenly felt guilty about Jill and decided instantly to drop her, deciding instantly again not to be so . . . 'foolish' was the word that came first into my mind.

We'd finished coffee. "I still see my husband. I can stand a week every month or so . . . I even like going . . . that's not true. I'm glad to go. But I'm also glad to come away after a few days."

"I'd like to meet them," I said.

"Everybody in England would like to meet them . . . in the world." Jane raised her arms expansively.

Alistair looked at me, meaning that if I wanted to meet them then Jane was the way. I tried to work out how scrupulous I was prepared to be . . . unscrupulous I suppose I meant. Alistair asked her:

"Do I remember correctly . . . are you going into Leeds this afternoon?"

She nodded.

"Do you mind dropping Tony? I've got to get over to Carlisle and it would help me a lot." He turned to me: "You can get home from Leeds on your own, can't you?"

I nodded easily, pleased at the smoothness of our behaviour. Jane looked at me quizzically.

She walked with him to the gate. They stood talking there for a short time, looking back at me once or twice, then he kissed her and went to his car, still parked at the church.

I sat on the lawn, eyes closed, face into the sun. I smelt her perfume but didn't open my eyes. She asked me if I was in a hurry to go to Leeds.

"I've got to be home for the weekend. I'm taking the kids out," I said. There was a seasoned, furtive quality about our voices.

"I'm glad you find me attractive," she said.

I opened my eyes. She was sitting very close. We looked at each other, anticipating our actions. She said, "Alistair's very nice.

He went to prison when he was younger. He killed someone in a brawl in a pub. He was an assistant lecturer at Leeds University at the time. He reckons it did him good . . . prison I mean."

"Is he married?"

"I can never make it out. He lives with his brother, Donald, the painter."

She paused. "You must've heard of him, he's very successful." I shook my head. 'Well, they live together with someone called Rachel. There's a son, he's in his teens. I think Donald's the father of the boy, but it doesn't seem to matter."

I don't know what Jane had said that caused this, but at that moment I tingled all over, for an instant glimpsing a kind of huge exciting process of which we were all part. A good, massive, reassuring Plan. I asked, "Do you feel we're all—Alistair, you, me, your family—part of some benign process that's indifferent to us?"

She looked at me, alarmed, defensive. "Not you as well!" she said. She got up and walked inside. I watched her, considered following her, then decided that wasn't part of the Plan. I closed my eyes and gave myself to the sun.

Days later, Jane, her car and I crossed over to France on the Hovercraft. It was a bright day. The sea was flat. We stood at the bar. She said, "You've got to give it to my husband, he made it as a writer."

"I enjoyed his books. Er . . . will he mind?"

"About us?" I nodded. "Not unless you make it obvious. That's how free the great man is," she said without mockery.

She drove fast along the Autoroute to Beauvais. I was excited and apprehensive. She avoided Beauvais and about fourteen kilometres further on we came to a high, green scarp. She turned off right and followed the winding road to the top. We had to pass through a huge farmyard—dogs barking and something one rarely sees these days, even in France, hens, ducks, geese pecking about the place. Her husband came to greet us. I looked at him, embarrassed. In the film of Mary's interview he was an implacable, aggressive figure. Now he was assured, looking too young, too vigorous to be Jane's husband. He indicated her cases:

"Help me will you. You're Tony Foster. I'll call you Tony if I may. You know who I am."

He made sure Jane was well on her way to their house, then, "Look, there's something I'd like to get out of the way before we start to know each other. I know Jane and you are probably lovers . . . I hope so anyway. But not here, you understand. I'm hoping . . ." He looked at me keenly, a slight smile about his eyes, ". . . she'll sleep with me . . . I insist on some husbandly rights. She likes to pretend I don't want to know. It sounds complicated but it doesn't have to be." I nodded, very embarrassed. He added, "She's always been a good wife, a good person to be with. Thank God she stuck it out." He glanced shrewdly at me. I fumbled for a coherent word but found none.

A Boy with very long hair came up to us. He was naked. His limbs were slender, his skin a delicate brown, almost gold. He moved with feminine grace, his feet kind of feeling the texture of the ground. He looked about eleven years old, though his intense, quiet eyes and great tranquility of manner were of someone much older. I wanted to devour him with my eyes, but when he smiled at me I noticed I turned abruptly away. I heard him say to his grandfather, "I want to learn to read."

"Has Mary said anything about that?"

"She thought I might like to discuss it with you."

"Why me? I don't think *you'll* get much from books. All good books are the same . . . say the same thing. Why don't you ask this young man what he thinks? He's a teacher."

I had to look at the Boy now. "I'm not a teacher any more," I said.

"I'm a learner," his grandfather said.

"I'm a learner, as well," I blurted out.

The Boy examined me quickly, then seemed to go into himself.

Immediately I was reminded of Mary. He took one of the cases and walked towards the house.

At dinner there was just Jane, Anthony and I. I ate very little.

"Why didn't he learn to read, Mr Johnson?"

"Don't call me Mr Johnson. 'Doctor Johnson' if you want to make fun of me, otherwise, 'Anthony'. Since I made it, everybody quite properly calls me Anthony."

He looked warmly at Jane. She smiled straight into his eyes. "Except Jane of course, she calls me anything."

"Why wasn't he taught to read, Anthony?" I asked uncomfortably.

"He seemed not to want to learn. Mary leaves all his decisions to him. He can *speak* as many languages as we know between us."

I said, "You told the Boy that he won't get much from books. That's the opposite of my experience." At the back of my mind I suddenly glimpsed the possibility that my education had been worthless. "Most of what I know comes from books."

Anthony looked at me for a little while, his eyes bright and mischievous.

"I told *him* he wouldn't get much from books. You and I, we need books like a diabetic needs insulin . . . you see?"

"What's his name?" I asked.

"He hasn't got one yet . . . I see you're shocked. Mary wants him to choose his own."

"I'm not shocked," I said, not exactly honestly.

Jane and Anthony wanted to be on their own that night, so I drove her car into Beauvais and broke my diet by drinking half a bottle of fine claret. I wandered round the town—destroyed twice, except for the cathedral and two other substantial medieval buildings, during the 39–45 war. It had been rebuilt in a totally undistinguished, well-planned way. It was a relief to walk through the depressing streets and come upon the great cathedral with her flying buttresses. I sat in a café watching the evening strollers. Jane and Anthony drove up and parked near the cathedral. At first Anthony wanted to take Jane in, but she insisted on leading him into the centre of the town.

When I got back I found a tall, well-dressed man of about my own age. He looked at me carefully then held out his hand:

"Christopher Arden-Jones . . . you must be Tony Foster."

I accepted his hand, assenting.

"Mary's with the Boy . . . care for a glass of wine?"

Without thinking I accepted. He gave me bits of cheese with the wine and we sat, sipping at our glasses, quite at ease for more than half an hour. Little was said. I was relaxed, a bit muzzy and quite happy not to talk. Something about Christopher was reassuring. His style I suppose. Also, when he moved it was with confidence, elegance and economy. Eventually he said, "You're the first stranger we've seen here for some time. In fact we have few visitors. A friend of mine . . . he's a retired Anglican bishop . . . comes over pretty regularly. So does Seymore-Cartwright. You know who I mean . . . your . . . our psychiatrist."

"How is he?"

"Well. Very well. He sees Jane quite a bit."

Christopher brought over the bottle and filled my glass. He went on: "He rarely talks about his patients, you know, but he has mentioned you from time to time."

I leaned forward, keen to ask what Seymore-Cartwright had found to say. Christopher smiled, almost to himself: "I suppose you'd like to know what he said? He didn't break any professional rules that I know of . . . confessional and all that. It's just that he seems to have found something in common between your . . . problems and mine. I'm speaking of when we were his patients."

I suddenly became aware of being unsettled. My hands were tense. Christopher looked at me in a very kindly way: "Do you happen to know anything about wine?" "Only that it's fattening," I answered. Instantly I felt foolish. He was quick to react: "Oh,

I'm terribly sorry . . . I didn't realise you're trying to get into shape."

I began to explain how my life had changed. He was very interested, particularly in the bits about David. I must've talked for an hour or so. He listened, asking questions occasionally. I remember the last thing he said was something about David and me getting out of prison at about the same time.

When I got to bed that night, I began to go to sleep straight away. But as I thought hazily about the day, my mind cleared itself and became active. I found myself explaining to Margaret, as if she was in bed with me, just what I wanted to do with my life.

"I want to take part in a vertical revolution," I told her. "It's useful but only peripherally so for students and workers to fight and kill and be killed. It's useless to point out the uselessness of work when there isn't any meaningful substitute for it for most people. To change society one must start by changing people. To change people one must start by changing child-rearing habits . . ."

"I wish someone had changed your mother's child-rearing habits," Margaret seemed to say, "she's got something to answer for."

A John Lennon song from the early seventies jingled through my mind:

"Mother,
You had me but I never had you . . ."

"It's sickness. All you men are the same," Margaret articulated salaciously. I went on for most of the night, trying to explain to her that I felt called to some great purpose . . . one of those called. "What purpose? Just explain. I want to understand." Her voice was mocking. "That's what I've got to find out." "You look in the wrong places," she said. We both knew where she meant. This was the kind of conversation we had never had while living together. She was great.

When I eventually slept my dreams were violent. I was dominated by cold, sexless women with smiling faces. "God is a mother" they pronounced flatly. I wanted to disagree. I fell over, struggling under their weight.

About ten o'clock I heard voices outside my window. My bedroom was on the ground floor.

I sat up in bed and looked out.

A Frenchman with his son, a delicate youth of about twelve, was talking painfully slow English to Anthony Johnson.

"Speak French, Monsieur," Anthony said.

Then, after the usual formal greetings one hears when Frenchmen speak to strangers, the Frenchman launched into a voluble account of how his son had had seizures . . . epileptic seizures . . .

I didn't follow his French too well—I'm not so good at the language, and he was speaking in a patois that I had never heard—but I gathered that something of the unusual qualities of Anthony's grandson—". . . votre petit-fils aux qualités impressionantes . . ." had attracted him. Recently, his son had met the Boy and Madame Johnson in Beauvais. The two boys had spoken to each other. They had touched. Since that day there had been no seizure.

"C'était un miracle."

Anthony listened politely but he seemed somehow angry. I thought he might rebuff the Frenchman but all he said was, "I don't know about 'miracle' but my grandson will be pleased . . . I'll go and send him out."

The boys recognised each other immediately. They approached, the French boy embarrassed but holding out his hands. His father was also embarrassed but followed his son and launched into a long, increasingly excited speech about the miraculousness of what had happened. The Boy nodded politely to the Frenchman but took little notice of what he said. He stood, facing the other boy, holding both his hands. The Frenchman slowly stopped talking, ending in the middle of a sentence. His embarrassment was acute and he glanced round nervously to make sure he wasn't being watched. Our eyes met. He became agitated. He spoke curtly to his son, almost bowed to the Boy, and hurried to his car parked a short distance from the house. The boys smiled at each other, both now very open to each other. They glanced towards the Frenchman.

I lay back as on a golden bed in some ancient myth. I gazed about, my eyes not connecting with the surfaces around me. There was a kind of glow inside my body. My intestines and bowels irradiated internal warmth.

I remember sighing deeply, sighing myself into deeper and deeper acceptance of what has been called the benign indifference of the universe.

I emerged at about four in the afternoon, and found that there was no-one in the house except Christopher who sat reading 'Process and Reality' at the tea table.

"Make some more tea," he said to me.

I took the teapot and found my way into the kitchen. I tried to explain in words my golden experiences. He seemed a bit upset. This made me feel very unsure. There was a longish pause. He was thinking of what to say. I waited.

"You shouldn't be so cynical," he finally murmured.

"It's a complete surprise to me that I was."

"You spoke quite bitterly."

"But I've been a dreamer for a long time now. I value my dreams . . . daydreams. When I was ill . . . even before that . . . I used to dream . . . 'chasing after moonbeams' my wife called it."

Neither of us spoke for a while. Christopher broke the silence:

"When I was ill I used to see a winsome little boy staring at everything. All around him things disintegrated . . . blew up and down and out. Each time something went he flinched. I used to stop my mind. It took me an awfully long time to learn to face up to the disintegration. Mary always said I would grow out of it . . . grow into the good part of my mind . . . you know, become the little boy . . . but I couldn't understand her. I used to stop my ears. I still don't believe her, but I listen more . . ."

"She must be unusual."

"Her father calls her an emotional aristocrat. I'm not frightfully sure what that means."

"What does he think of her?"

"You shouldn't ask me that . . . I remember once he told her she was the sum of what was crucially missing in all the women he'd ever known. I believe he meant, what they felt was missing in themselves . . . I never like reporting other people's ironies . . ."

"Was it an irony?"

"I hope so," Christopher said.

"I've read his novels."

"Did you like them? I find them insidious . . . even complacent. I can see they were necessary."

"Because of their religious themes?"

"Not really. I think because of their mythic quality."

"You mean they're preoccupied with churches and sex," I observed.

"Sex," he said, "the royal road to what Anthony wouldn't know whether to call 'wholeness' or 'holiness'."

"I first saw him in that interview Mary gave to the BBC."

"That was disturbing."

It was the following day that I met Mary. I was writing and had left my door open. She came in carrying clean sheets. We stood, kind of naked, looking at each other. Neither of us was uneasy. We looked over each other at leisure. I felt completely relaxed and open.

"We meet at last," she said matter-of-factly. "It's as if we've been avoiding each other."

"Not consciously so far as I'm concerned."

"I remember walking with you in the hospital grounds. I was carrying the Boy."

I didn't want to do more than assent. She went over to the bed and changed the sheets. I just watched her. The way she moved. The shape of her body. The colour of her skin and hair.

She said, "We didn't have anything to say to each other then. It was rather nice."

"Oh, I've a lot to say to you now."

She stopped what she was doing and looked around for somewhere to sit.

"You're not busy?" I asked.

She looked steadily at me, making the slightest negative movement of her head.

I couldn't think how to start. She smiled. I observed,

"I feel a bit disreputable here, in such serene company."

She shook her head slightly, as if erasing what I'd said from her mind.

"It's just that . . . I recently realised how useless my life has been . . . my style of life . . . the person I used to want to be. I decided to change. I started to lose weight, for example . . ."

She was listening attentively.

". . . I've given up my work . . . I've encouraged my wife and kids to leave me and live on their own . . ."

I couldn't think of what to say next.

She waited. I blurted out: "To use one of your father's terms, I've started fucking around . . ."

"My mother's also," she said. This reference to my relationship with Jane didn't make me feel uncomfortable. I looked into her eyes. They were enquiring, not cold, warm but somehow a long way away.

"You're telling me these things as if you want me to judge you."

"I want something from you," I heard myself say.

"Then you must learn how to take it."

"I would like to kiss you."

I was a little boy talking. The words came out of my mouth, completely surprising me.

"I like being kissed," she said simply, "and touched."

I was astounded. I became aware, gradually, of a strong intention to approach her body.

She stood up. Her dress was loosely buttoned down the front. I was very confident. A new feeling.

I don't remember the sequence of events. I unbuttoned her dress. She wore only pants underneath. She took them off. We each drew the other to ourselves. I remember being on my knees, my mouth against her belly, crying quietly. I could hear the familiar noises—the liquid squelchings and squeezings as soggy masses were muscled around inside her, the bump-bump of her solar pulse—and again I was part of a red-gold dream. Vaguely I remember her saying, "You lay in your bed last night unable to sleep. Your body torn . . ."

She looked down, like a madonna in one of Michelangelo's paintings, and lifted my head up.

". . . you're learning to live with your guilts."

I remember her body was firm and urgent. She enjoyed me.

I had a necessary orgasm.

We lay on my bed for an hour or so.

I cried, talked, dreamed aloud.

I remember kissing her sex endlessly . . . ploughing deep kisses into the entrance to her body.

As she was fastening her dress, Christopher popped his head round the still-open door.

"Oh there you are Mary," he said, waving in a friendly way to me, "there's something I would like you t . . t . . to do for me."

I watched him put his arm lightly round her shoulders as they walked towards the farmyard.

"What made you become a teacher?" the Boy asked later. We were walking away from the house.

"A kind of ignorance."

"Everything is ignorance . . . everything we know I mean."

I waited for him to continue.

"I try to unlearn it," he said.

"Unlearn everything?"

He nodded seriously. "It leads me back to why things were learned."

"I can't remember learning to be a teacher."

"Did you learn to think of yourself as a teacher?"

"I must've done." I was thinking of why I hadn't wanted to be a teacher. Endless reasons.

"Did the children in your classes affect you?"

"They wanted me to show them what to do, and then help them do it."

"They wanted you to do that, so you did it."

"I'd seen my teachers do it for me. I didn't do exactly what my teachers did but . . ."

"Did you do exactly what the children wanted you to do?"

"It was a mixture," I said. "What they wanted, what my teachers had done, and what I wanted to do."

"But you can't remember it?"

"Not learning it. I don't think I ever consciously decided about it. It followed from what was happening and what had happened."

"I'm being brought up to be a learner, not a teacher," he said. "Look." A kestrel had caught his eye. He pointed. The hawk dropped without noise, hovering at the crucial moment, talons seizing its prey. A slight scream. The hawk fluttered purposefully, absorbed in its actions, then looped its fierce hooked beak to its victim.

"Terrible," I said quietly.

"Do you think beautiful things stop because of killing?"

We walked in silence. He added after a few minutes, "Killing stops and starts things, doesn't it."

I nodded.

We started to talk again about my being a teacher. He asked if I knew how information was processed by the mind.

"I'm not informed on information theory," I joked.

"But it was information you got from other teachers and from the children that programmed what you did as a teacher."

"I got it quite unconsciously."

"You mean without knowing it your mind collected a lot of

information, analysed it, then told itself what to do, all the time changing as fresh information came in."

"That's right. But not much changing, I'm afraid. That's one of the reasons I gave it up."

The rarefied atmosphere began to weigh down on me. That's not right. It was the wearing effect of the lack of kind of gravity, the constant high-flying-experience of living with the Johnsons, that made me feel light-headed, unsure, confused even. I was used to the wretched world of everyday life where problems for much of the time are over there in another country, or in other people. And where spirituality and saintliness kept their distance. I remember being hungry for the chance to see the news. They didn't take newspapers nor had they a television. So I borrowed Jane's car and went into Beauvais.

I was highly anxious as I searched for a bar with television. It was strangely consoling to see the usual clips of urban war in America and violent picketing in Scotland. Even the stately European Congress of Trade Unions . . . the Yorkshire Miners' Representative dressed up like a Montague Burton's dummy having a stab at speaking French, was lovely. I found it all fascinating and reassuring. The Religious Pop-Festival was good. Easy to take. It had lasted all night followed by a wild communion-service at dawn with couples taking holy bread-and-wine before publicly having intercourse. Then the usual arrests by police equipped for dealing with terrorists rather than lovers. I left the bar vastly relieved.

Jane made me take her to Yorkshire the next morning. Inconsequentially, I was reluctant to leave. I'd only just started to get to know them and still hadn't really found out anything. There was an icy quality to Jane's insistence. "You can always come again," she said.

"Would they mind?"
"Ask them."

There was rioting in Boulogne. Good old reality. Helicopters, television crews, armoured personnel carriers, nasty explosions punctuated by rifle fire. We were diverted and missed the Hovercraft we'd booked for. Instead of leaving Boulogne at eleven we were there until two in the afternoon. As we bounced away from the harbour, there was still occasional rifle-fire.

I radio-phoned Alistair Shuttleworth from the Hovercraft, arranging for him to call to see me that evening. He was very keen to know about the Johnsons.

Margaret video-phoned just after I got home: "I'm depressed, feeling sorry for myself. And I know now that I hate you," she said.

I thought she was joking. She went on, "You've destroyed my life. I've give you my best years and . . . I hope you're satisfied."

"Are you having your period?"

This annoyed her. She shouted . . . she didn't care who heard . . . her life was finished . . . until I got all that bloody nonsense into my head, we'd had everything that life can offer . . . why wasn't I like other men? They had their affairs and kept it at that. She must've been a rotten wife or no good in bed . . . that's what was so crazy, we'd made love the night she left . . . speaking for herself it was good, better than good . . . she wanted to know what was going on . . . I waited, then reminded her, "All that was only half of it. The other half was that we both made each other behave badly. We were ugly with each other." She cut in, shouting again, "All marriages are ugly at times . . . that's what's so worthwhile, putting up with it, learning to live with it. Not flitting from one unreal affair to another. I know about Jill. She's pretty . . . sexy . . . young. I don't know what the Union of Teachers will think when they hear you're living with her but believe me, she's too intelligent to get stuck with you. She'll leave you . . . then you'll know how I feel."

"You didn't have to go. And I'm not living with her."

"Is she there now?"

"Of course she isn't."

"When you see her, tell her I'd like to speak to her."

"Why should she want . . ."

"Tell her."

Jill arrived later in the day, looking tired. Very much as if she'd been to work. She was glad to see me. She explained that much had happened. David had got a job in a café. Only a few days after he'd started work, a gang of youths in a couple of old, piston-engined cars had parked outside and started messing about. Jill had got involved—they'd pulled her about. David came out to tell them to clear off. There'd been a fight . . . a terrible fight, and David had been arrested, brought before magistrates, and remanded in the cells. She'd been to see him. He'd asked her to get in touch with me.

She also had problems. She'd been excluded from school for reasons that she said were not clear, and had left home. David had suggested she could sleep at my house and she'd been there two nights. Margaret's comments began to make more sense.

"I'm working in David's café now."

"Which bed did you sleep in?"

"Yours. But I can sleep in David's tonight if . . ."

"Have you been seeing much of David?"

"I like him. He's lovely and pure . . . like innocent."

"He's got damn cold eyes, even when he's smiling."

"I don't know," she disagreed.

Alistair hesitated when he saw Jill. I introduced them and she said she was tired and went to bed. I listened, trying to hear if she was going into my bed which was immediately over where I was sitting. Alistair noticed and looked up expressively.

"Nice girl," he said warmly. "Is this her furniture?" He indicated the battered chairs that I presumed David had bought.

"I don't quite know. When I went away there was nothing in this room and a friend called David in the house. I come back to find chairs, Jill living here, and David in the local prison for assault."

"And you're complaining!"

The bed above my head creaked.

Alistair said, "I spent some time in prison for assault. Did Jane tell you?"

I nodded.

"I remember standing in the dock, looking up at the judge . . . at Leeds Assizes . . . telling him that I was up there with him, sitting in judgement on myself. He listened, I'll give him that. I sentenced myself to a long term. He only gave me nine months . . . only! How much did Jane tell you?"

"No more than that. Less. What's it like killing a man?"

"Like hitting him very hard. He was putting a pint-glass of bitter to his mouth as I swung. The glass was smashed into his neck."

Alistair showed me the jagged scars on his fist.

"None of us knew how to stop him bleeding."

We sat drinking. Eventually he asked how I got on with Jane.

"Very well. I spent a few days with her, then I came over here to spend an afternoon with the kids. That evening, she picked me up and we got the first Hovercraft on Tuesday morning."

"What are they all like?"

"Mary and the Boy are . . . they both ought to be absolutely impossible but they're . . ." I paused trying to think what to say. Words like 'saintly' and 'serene' came into my mouth but they seemed trite.

"That's very clear. Start with Anthony Johnson."

"Haven't you been?"

"Jane only takes her lovers."

"Oh!"

"Anthony, you know, got around a lot when they were younger. Jane either didn't want to or felt she shouldn't for his sake—she says both at different times. Now she gets around when he can't . . ."

Alistair gestured expressively. "It's quite important for her to take her boyfriends."

"Oh!"

"How was he with you?"

"Even better now I know that, though I thought he was great. She told me to pretend we weren't lovers. The first thing he did was to tell me to pretend he didn't know but he hoped we were . . ."

Alistair was delighted. He slapped his thighs repeatedly, hooted with laughter, and kept saying. "That's bloody marvellous. Isn't it?" Each time he asked I had to agree.

"What's the Boy like?"

"He often looks like a girl . . . you know, his movements, the way he kind of organises the position of his body . . . he sleeps in the same bed as Mary and Christopher."

"If I'd done that all my problems would've been solved."

"You'd be a gibbering idiot," I said.

"I think if I'd slept with my mother . . . it would've been marvellous for all of us. Unless, of course, she'd taken my brother Donald in as well."

"You'd 've been a gibbering idiot."

"Donald thinks it's oedipal problems that attract us to each other. He thinks there's a masonry of free spirits . . . he's the painter . . ."

He waited to see if I wished to comment, then, ". . . people who've got free from the inhibitions built up in them by their parents. Mainly men. You met a couple of women in London, Sybil and Emma, but mostly men."

"Those two girls . . . they were a bit ominous."

"They organise pop-festivals. Damn cold fucks but they make a lot of money."

"Really?"

"They've got good minds. Good Oxford minds. They're rich and yet very, very revolutionary."

"Are they going to work in Beauvais as well?"

"I doubt it. But they're interested in Mary Johnson. If the

Boy's what he might be, then they'll promote him and if they promote him, everybody everywhere will know about him."

I heard Jill moving in my bed. Alistair also heard it and looked keenly at me. I remember easing forward in my chair. He thought I wanted to end the conversation and began to talk quickly to keep it going. "You'll probably meet them again soon. They're interested in the England end of the thing. You don't really know what I'm talking about but you must've realised that you're getting into something that's been preparing itself for some time."

I glanced involuntarily at my watch. He went on, "Have you noticed how committed and partisan the news commentators are on telly these days?"

I shook my head. "Does it matter?" My mind was upstairs. Alistair thought it would matter if so-called 'fiction' and 'fact' could be presented as two aspects of the same unity. "Mary's living a fiction. I don't give a shit where she got it from . . . her father's novels or wherever. She and that Boy of hers are occupying the oldest story in the world. It's been told a million times across cultures and across time. And they *are* the story. See what I mean? Instead of the whole of Europe watching East Germany play England, or the European Song Contest, they could be watching that Boy of Mary's . . . if he's worth watching."

"But who's to decide?"

He glanced up at the ceiling, then said, trying to control his excitement, "It's entirely up to Mary in the first place. If she does what's she's doing well, then she'll attract people like me and those terrible Oxford twins. And we'll attract the World. It won't take two hundred years to get to Rome this time. It's been done before and . . ." He stopped. His ambitions for Mary were immense. I felt suitably small. My keenest ambition at that moment was to get into bed with Jill. Alistair looked into my face. He tried to hide his disappointment: "Tonight's not the night, but I want to know a good deal more about your reaction to the Johnsons."

"Can I come and see you soon?" I asked, trying not to sound dismissive.

"First things first, you old bugger," he said, "I've given you a lot to think about." He smiled, discontented with the evening, clasping his legs and drawing them up to his chest. He glanced at his watch and jumped up, walking quickly out of the room.

I got to the front door as his car whined out of the drive.

I visited David briefly the next morning. He told me to go and see the police Superintendent and say that if the charge was reduced from grievous bodily harm to common assault, he would plead guilty. The Superintendent wasn't surprised by the offer, merely agreeing to pass on the information to the Chief Constable. I tried to explain how important it was for David not to go back to prison. The Superintendent smiled, offered me a cigar, and said, "I take your point, Mr Foster. I shouldn't worry if I were you."

He lit his cigar, puffed and smiled again: "He's got a lot of form but my boys like him. It'll do him no harm to think he's being done for g.b.h. for another day or two. Do you get my meaning?" It was very obvious, now he'd explained, and we smiled at each other conspiratorially.

"These small-town bogies 've got no imagination," David told me when I went back to see him. "I could bust out of this fucking nick in no time if I really thought they were going to send me down. I did them a favour."

"The thing to do is keep cool," I said weakly.

"Did he agree to common assault?"

I shook my head. David looked closely at me, trying to probe the rather silly fixed expression on my face.

"The Superintendent didn't take me into his confidence," I lied.

"What did he say?"

"It wasn't up to him."

"It isn't. It's up to the Chief Constable. Well, it's a bugger if I've got to go down again for helping your girl friend. An' I 'aven't even been there meself."

He knew he'd upset me. I remember trying to smile.

"I'm sorry, Tony."

I shrugged, feeling very exposed.

"You know me . . . I'm just a rough lad . . ."

I held up my hand, wanting him to stop.

". . . though I must be about the only bugger who hasn't been there."

Neither of us spoke for two minutes. He looked at me, defiantly.

"Why do you have to say things like that?" I asked.

"I dunno."

"I realise now you fancy Jill . . ."

He palmed me down.

Silence.

"I suppose I wanted to 'urt you," he said.

That was a good thing to say. "That's why I like you, David, because you can say things like that."

Silence. He asked, "Tell me straight. Am I going down?"

"No, you're not. But they're going to keep you guessing for another day or two."

"I knew you were fannying," he said with relief.

"They think it'll do you good."

"It will now, knowing that."

"You'll have to be careful."

"Listen, you've no need to worry. These bogeys are amateurs compared with the bastards I've been up against in the big cities."

"When you talk like that you worry me."

"You've nothing to worry about."

"I know I'm a bit of a nervous maiden aunt, but I wish you'd try and think about how other people think and feel."

He looked at me with a certain contempt.

"I don't know why I bother with you," he said.

We both smiled, each thinking different thoughts, I imagine.

David was bailed out by the café proprietor the following Monday. The two of them went on a drinking bout that started the minute they got out of the magistrate's court, about ten-thirty in the morning, and lasted until about eleven at night, at which time I was just about to follow Jill up to bed.

David came in, reeling, followed by his boss who was concerned that David was put to bed out of harm's way. I gave the necessary assurances and we were left alone.

I made some coffee and went into the sitting room.

" 'Ow do you like the chairs I bought for you?"

"Great."

"Do you know, I must've propositioned ten birds tonight and not 'ad a taker. What's 'appening in the world?"

I was impatient and wanted to get to bed.

"An' I could really love a bird tonight . . . you know, really put a lot of love into one."

I stood up.

"You're a bad-tempered bugger, sit down and let's have a chat . . . we've not seen each other for weeks."

I sat down.

"That's better . . . now, 'ow did your trip to France go?"

"Well."

He grinned.

"When are you goin' back . . . I'm not pushing you away, like."

I suddenly realised that if I went away again I was leaving Jill in the same house.

"This is your 'ouse. She's your bird. But I don't know what you expect of her. She's crazy about you."

"I know."

"I wish you'd try and think about how other people feel," he said. I looked across at him, angrily. We looked into each other's eyes.

"Come off it, Tony. You know I wouldn't even try and touch her. I swear on my mother's grave."

"Your mother isn't dead."

"I would swear, honest."

He was laughing at me. Quite rightly.

"Is she up there now?" he asked.

I looked at him.

"You're playing with me, David."

"You're such a fucking idiot at times—I don't mean you 'aven't got brains . . . I sometimes wonder where your brains are, but I never doubt you've got 'em . . . never. At least, not often."

"You're enjoying yourself. You're quite right. I'm silly about that girl."

"She's a very nice girl, do you know that?"

"She's good."

"She's very unhappy, you know." He spoke seriously.

"I think I know. She's going to university in October. She'll enjoy that."

"She told me she wants to stay here."

I looked at him with interest.

"Don't tell her I told you, but that's what she said. It's something to do with her stepfather cutting off her allowance."

I put my head in my hands.

"Her mother sounds to be as big a bitch as mine . . . bigger, because her mother's educated and ought to know better."

I remembered Jill saying that she didn't want to get involved with me.

"Your missus came 'ere and gave 'er a good going-over . . . if I 'adn't been here I don't know what would've happened."

"Margaret came here?"

"Gave Jill a right going over. I don't know what they see in you."

"Look," I said, "I'm just going up to Jill for a minute. I'll be straight back."

He looked at me, his cold eyes weighing up the chances of my not coming back.

I leaned over Jill. She was half-asleep.

"You're a lovely girl, Jill. I love you."

She looked up at me, surprised.

"I just wanted to come up and tell you I love you. I've promised

David I'll go back and have a chat. Go to sleep, love."

She leaned up to be kissed, then settled in the bed.

"I've been sitting here, waiting for you, finking about my old woman . . . you know, I put everything that's 'appened to me down to her."

"I used to like her."

"Everybody liked her. She went out of her way to be liked. I loved 'er, I still love her. But there are times when I feel that the most important thing in my life is to get hold of a shooter and go and do her in. Strange, innit? And yet even while I tell you that, I can remember dreaming about her and me, sitting by a crystal-clear river, she's combing my hair and taking sleep out of my eyes, an' I'm the 'appiest little bugger alive."

"She's either a perfect mother or a perfect witch."

He looked at me, suddenly sober.

"That's it. She's the only person that can make me feel really small. And the only one that can make me feel ten feet tall. You know that? The only one."

He thought for a bit. "She's like two separate people. And so am I."

"What about your father?"

"You saw more of 'im than I did. Whenever he came on leave I took off didn't I . . . and stayed away until he went back. He was killed in 1970, in the fighting in Belfast. They 'ad a state funeral for him. I was in Wormwood Scrubs at the time. I could've gone. They offered me but I turned it down. It would've been great being outside for four days but I told them to fuck off. They offered me the travel warrant and a voucher for money but I told them to stuff 'em. I hated the bastard . . . hated him."

He sounded the aitches heavily.

"What you're saying is that you're a petty thief because . . ."

He cut in, "I'm not a petty fief."

"Sorry. I'm not trying to hurt you, David, I'm trying to get straight in my own mind what you've been saying. You're the person you are . . . you know, you've approached ten women tonight and had no takers . . . because of your parents."

He nodded, his eyes wide open.

"Can you consider becoming a different person?"

"Why should *I* change? Fuck 'em. They've made me what I am . . . they've got to put up with me. I'm not staying 'ere long, I can tell you."

He felt he had said too much. He looked at me quickly to see if I'd noticed.

"You mean you're still bent?"

"Not bent, but I don't intend to spend the rest of my life working in a café."

"And getting turned down ten times every night."

"Aye," he said.

"It doesn't have to be a café."

"Whatever it is, I'm the mug."

"Compared to the mug you've been?"

"I like this straight talk . . . but it never gets us anywhere . . . you've got everything your own way now, but I knew you when you were a nutter. All credit to you for getting yourself straightened out . . ."

"What about you?"

"You fink I'm a nutter?" he asked, studying my face. He went on, "It's easy to say that from where you stand . . . if you'd been inside . . ."

I remember cutting into him, "Just to get the facts straight, David, not to win a point, I was inside . . . being in that bloody mental hospital . . . psychiatric hospital . . . was being inside . . . I was five months there. They wanted me to have electric shock . . . they told me, when I could bear to listen, that they could cure me . . . help me . . . they thought that electric violence could calm my violence. I told them no . . . I told them I prefer to deal with my own problems. They insisted, I stuck out . . . they brought in specialists. I told them no. I wanted to crouch in my bed, in that ward, away from everybody, just bearing with what was going on inside me . . . being submerged by it . . . finding myself again on the surface, refusing to think I was other than responsible to myself for what was happening . . . insisting, for as long as I could each time, that I was mad . . . confused . . . lost . . . and that any sense I was to make of myself had to be kind of through it all . . . I don't know."

"Clever bugger, aren't you," he said intelligently.

"I'm being a bit precious, aren't I?"

David looked around, went over to the mantelpiece and took one of my cigars, lit it, puffed, sat down.

He said, "We're the same, you and me. When I was going out of my nut I used to demand . . . demand my rights . . . to be locked in my cell. I put the 'ole fucking nick in Coventry . . ."

I laughed.

"I can imagine you and me . . . probably at the same time, each locked in our crazy heads . . . putting the whole world in Coventry."

"But I'm not as clever as you," he said, looking at me cunningly, "you've . . ."

I waited, He flicked his cigar.

"You've wangled everything to suit you . . . made it all look good. Your wife and kids are just up the road . . . you love them . . . Jill's living here and paying you rent . . . you love her."

"You're living here also . . . and paying no rent that I know of . . . and I love you too . . ."

We both laughed, each uncertain of the other's feelings.

David stood up, thinking about each word:

"There's always a big brain behind really big jobs . . . crimes. They're the ones who go to dinner with the Chief Constable, know the Mayor and all the local politicians. They never get pinched . . . it's poor little cunts like me that get pinched."

"You've been reading too many detective stories."

"Well, what kind of stories have you been reading?" he asked, sarcastically.

"You think I'm a kind of crook."

"Well look at you . . . you've got everything going for you and you've not been touched . . . it's Margaret who's hurt . . . your kids. It'll be Jill next."

"How would you know if I'm hurt?"

"Me, I'm just saying how it appears to me like. Not only me."

He leered, his face ugly with the anger he was controlling.

"Look, David, I'm trying to recognise myself . . . trying to grow."

"So is Margaret, and your bloody kids, and Jill . . . but they're all being knocked. You're growing all right but what about them?"

"If I can grow, then those I love might have a better chance to grow as well." As I spoke I sensed the weakness of what I said.

"I can only tell you 'ow it seems to me," he said, pointing at me with his cigar, "you're conning them. All the time. That's what I think anyway . . . I may be wrong."

I stood up, facing him.

"Listen," I said, "it isn't just me loving them and their being hurt . . . it's everybody locked in their cells trying to love each other and themselves . . . love each other as themselves . . . but they're all locked in. They demand to be locked in because that's the only way they know not to burst with what they feel. I refuse to be locked in my cell. It's a choice I've made. All those I love have got to live with my choice, as I try to live with theirs. They choose to be confined. I choose not to be."

He shouted, his face white: "But *you've* chosen not to live with Margaret and your kids."

"Margaret chose that . . . not to live with me if I was . . ."

I stopped, choked by the realisation that he'd been talking to Margaret.

He said, "She didn't choose. That's exactly it . . . you forced her to leave so your nose would be clean . . . that's what I mean . . . you conned her, you're conning her all the time."

"Don't use your cheap little mind to try to understand what I'm about."

"You're just another cunt like all the rest of us," he accused.

"You're just a cheap petty crook trying to see everything from a petty point of view."

"OK, I'm a crook, and I'm little. But I can be a little crook with a bit of style, carn' I?"

We stared at each other. David was trying to force a grin onto his face. His eyes were strained, feelingless, frightening. Jill came in, wrapped in a blanket. David turned to her, stared at her face, then went out, making a fierce, dismissive gesture. I wandered around the room, stiff, seething inside. She said:

"I like the way he stands up to you."

"When was Margaret here?"

"Oh, once I think."

"That wily little bastard's playing her off against me."

"I wish you'd stop calling him 'little'."

"Go to bed."

She gathered her blanket around her, looking into my face.

"Go on. I'm not angry. You're right. The little bastard does stand up to me. He gets through as well. I'm hurt."

"He's got to hurt you."

"I know. If he and Margaret . . . if he realises what that would do to me . . ."

Jill started to cry. She turned and went out.

I remember groaning. Out into the garden to groan . . . stretch . . . twist . . . grovel . . . all the time conscious of the need to modulate my movements and sounds to keep them to myself. The grass was wet, cold.

When I got into bed, Jill was wide awake. She said,

"What if he has me?"

"I know," I answered. "Do you want him to?"

She turned onto her side, pushing her bottom towards me. I turned to face her back, and tucked my thighs under hers. Neither of us moved except to shift a little from time to time as our bodies melted into sleep.

Small towns are small-minded. . . . This I'd always known, but seriously under-estimated. It was clear when I wandered about my business that those I counted on as, if not friends, understanding and thoughtful acquaintances, found it very difficult to accept what I was doing. Many dismissed my smiles with curt, even abrasive greetings that signalled simultaneously goodbye. Others enquired about Margaret, the kids, then 'your little girl'. When the conversation went any further, which increasingly I prevented, I was offered a succession of cynical, cruel, condescending bits of advice about soiling my own doorstep. I think one or two were genuinely concerned for my kids.

I met my eldest son, Michael, by accident one lunchtime. The natural thing to do was to invite him for a meal.

"No, thanks," he said, his voice tight. He glanced around, as if expecting hostile stares.

"How are things?"

"Better if you stayed away," he said.

"I can guess how difficult it is for you," I said.

"Can you?"

"Why don't you come round to the house one evening? We could talk . . . have a glass of beer."

"If you lived with us, you'd know I don't use alcohol . . ."

"What would we do then? I don't smoke pot."

"I'm off drugs," he said, "and Mummy doesn't want me to see you."

"She's angry. She'll get over it. She's a good girl."

"She might . . . I won't," he said. He walked away, his normally graceful body made ungainly by his feelings.

There followed three nights of huge agitations and rabid, morbid restlessness. I had to struggle not to be forced totally out of myself by the tensions and massive anxieties of my body. My head was knotted. So were the muscles of my throat and jaw. It was difficult to go on living.

"It's kind of you to see me so quickly," I said to Dr Seymore-Cartwright.

"Not at all. I hear you've been to Beauvais."

"Yes."

Small, self-contained in his leather chair, he looked out of the huge window. He said, "Er, I think you know I go there occasionally. I find Mary Johnson remarkable. The Boy obviously is marvellous. With a mother like that, and Christopher for a . . . I mustn't say 'father' because he's more a brother."

"The three of them sleep together."

"Always have."

Neither of us spoke. Then I said,

"One of my friends said that if he'd slept with his mother and father he would've solved all his problems."

"Not unless he happened to be blessed with parents like Mary and Christopher."

"That's what I said."

"I'm glad they invited you."

"Did you ask them to?"

"Oh no, I wouldn't consider making that kind of demand on them. I merely happened to know that you and Christopher might like to meet. It was Jane Johnson who arranged things."

He looked at me.

"My wife, Margaret, left me, took the kids up the road. I bought her a house."

"Up the road?"

"She chose it . . . it was her idea we should be close."

"You mean it was her idea and you didn't agree?"

"I agreed . . . still agree."

I went on to explain what had happened. Then I told him: "I've been fucking around . . . Jane Johnson took me, I gather, to show to her husband."

"Anthony is way above all that. He would understand. Didn't he try to reassure you?"

I assented. We both were smiling.

"He's splendid," I said.

"So is Jane. She's put up with him off and on for what is it . . . nearly forty years . . . and lasted him out."

"I feel, doctor, that I'm part of some huge plan. I know this is what your patients usually feel."

"And they're usually right. The plan is their family's, and it starts before birth. My most intractable patients are the sturdiest protagonists of the plan they feel damaged by."

I got up and walked around the room.

"What was my family's plan for me?"

He glanced through my file which he had on his desk. He said: "It doesn't matter . . . I could never find out anyway. You might, but it's unlikely. In some way, for some reason, they experienced you as not one of them."

"I've often felt that my mother had some special purpose for me, and kind of brought me up to fulfil it."

"You may be right, but I doubt it. Well, in fact you're certainly wrong . . . it never works out like that. It's more fundamental and unverbalised . . . unknown. My own parents . . ."

He stopped. We both smiled. I began to laugh.

My laughter got out of control and I ended up sobbing. He waited.

"I seem to have large gaps in my awareness," I said eventually.

"All the time?"

"I've got a girl living with me. She's lovely. One of my pupils."

I looked at him. He waited, relaxed.

"She's eighteen. Knows her own mind. We love each other. I just let her into my . . . house without even thinking about the effect on my children."

"Have they met her?"

"Not yet."

He offered, "They may like her. And your wife?"

"She . . . well, she obviously feels . . ."

He cut in: "You feel very guilty and wonder if you might be in some way relapsing."

"Well, not relapsing exactly because I always think of my illness as the beginning of my sanity."

"You feel that your sanity may be beginning again?"

We both smiled. He went on: "If you return to Beauvais, give them my fondest regards."

He got up and came round his desk.

I wanted to kiss him. He said, "Please feel free to ring anytime. Not just when you're upset."

"Before I slip away, can I ask you what you think of Mary?"

"She's the most wonderful person I've ever met. Christopher is very charming and elegant. But she's . . . well . . . miraculously sane."

"Is it dangerous?"

"Ah," he said, "that's another matter."

Jane Johnson wasn't pleased to see me.

"I was hoping I could stay with you for a day or two," I said.

"Why on earth didn't you ring?"

"You would've put me off."

She looked at me carefully, waiting to choose the most devastating words.

I beat her to it: "I want you."

She let me in.

"I don't mean body and soul."

She followed, quite uncertain.

I danced a kind of dance: asking the goddess for wisdom.

She was still undecided.

"Have you eaten?" I asked.

She shook her head.

"It would be great if you'd let me cook you a supper."

She frowned, mock-seriously.

"I've come all this way because I want you and I want to cook you a supper."

"Are you alright?"

"My sanity's beginning again."

She stepped away from me apologetically. I went on:

"I've been to see your friend Seymore-Cartwright."

Now she was alarmed.

"He thinks my sanity is beginning again. Do you see?"

"Stop this," she said firmly, the beginning of shrillness in her voice.

"I'm sorry. I'm frightening you."

I sat down. She looked at me then glanced towards the videophone in the hall.

"I'm alright. I'm a bit excited . . . relieved . . . depressed . . . expectant."

"I'm on my own. I don't think I should encourage you to stay."

"Please, Jane, I'll be alright."

"If you don't mind, I think I'll ring Alistair and ask him to come over."

I began to get up. She became very nervous. I sat back.

"That's probably a good idea," I said.

There was no reply from Alistair.

I went into the kitchen and began to look for food.

"You really did frighten me," she said after supper.

"I don't know quite what I intended . . . perhaps to frighten. I'm frightened of what's happening."

"What is happening?"

"I came here because I thought you knew."

"You mean you expect me to be able to tell you what's wrong with you?"

"Not that. But I want to know what you think is happening. You know, we've both talked before about a kind of huge plan of which we may all be part."

"You talked about a plan. I didn't."

"But you must know what Mary and Christopher and Anthony are doing."

"I don't pretend to know."

"Come on, Jane, they must've told you things."

"They've talked to me a lot. Not recently. But I remember that night when Mary told us—Christopher was here for supper, it was a Sunday evening—she was conceived of God. It sounded to me as if she'd suddenly invented him."

I said, "She ought to be crazy but she's miraculously sane."

Neither of us spoke for a bit then I asked, "What was your reaction?"

"You mean how did I feel? . . . I felt a lot of things. I felt it was the end of something very good. I felt that I'd always known it would happen. I felt terribly angry . . . terribly weak. I can't say what I felt."

"Did you believe her?"

"What? My own daughter?" She was heavily sarcastic.

"You must've believed her in a way . . . to feel all that . . . still feel it. What she said must have made some deep sense."

"Deep fucking nonsense. Of course I didn't believe it. I still don't. She's meddling with things that are far too big for her. She doesn't know what she's doing."

"But look how strongly it still makes you feel."

"Because I knew who the father was."

She was agitated.

I got her another drink.

"I'm alright," she said.

I wanted her to go on. She swallowed her drink.

"I know what they're doing . . . it's obvious. You know. They're bringing up my grandson to be God. It's fucking terrible."

"You like using the word 'fucking'."

"I believe in the word 'fucking'," she shouted.

She went towards the drink-cupboard. She turned:

"It's fucking terrible. They're destroying what chance the little bastard had of being normal . . . it's so cruel . . . downright, straightforward cruelty."

"But he's a beautiful child."

"Have you see him with other children?"

"Only once but . . ."

"There are things you don't know. Is it right for a child to sleep all his life, every night, with his mother and father?"

"Not with his father?"

"Yes, with his . . . oh . . . well, with Christopher and Mary. They're at it all the time. Mary believes in the word fucking. So does Christopher now . . . if you'd known him when he was Rector here . . . it's unbelievable. He baptised her, you know."

"And she baptised him."

She stared at me, uncomprehending. She went on:

"He was so polite and respectable. He called his shirts 'linen' and changed every day at least twice. He was so refined and withdrawn. Warm you know, but very introverted. Look at him now. Mary did that."

"He's good now."

"He was good then."

"You mean you preferred him then to what he is now."

"No," she said.

We both laughed. She was less tense.

"No, I'll give her that. He's more human now. I like him a lot. I suppose my husband would say I love him. It's terrible isn't it. We're like a nest of twining snakes."

"You're not very logical but I think I understand what you're saying."

"God," she announced, "isn't very logical. In fact he's totally illogical. And I know. He's my grandson."

"A lot of grandmothers think that."

She looked keenly at me, weighing up my mood.

"Do you want to sleep here?" she asked.

"Not with you," I answered slowly.

"Please yourself."

In bed I became disturbed. Then confused. I couldn't think why. I moved about the bed a lot, trying to sleep. I thought from time to time of going in to Jane, but some deeper impulse kept me away from her.

About four I got up. I wasn't sure where I was going until I got into the open air. It was just light and I could see the roof and tower of the church.

I wandered around the church. Its neglect troubled me. I sat in the dusty pews, then wandered round again. I tried a few doors and eventually found the cleaning equipment. Another search and I found the main switch for the electricity.

I began at the font, using the largest vacuum cleaner. I became totally absorbed in the work.

I suddenly became aware of the church lighting up. I glanced up at the East window. I think I had a black-out of some kind.

I began to think again a little later. The sun was still shining strongly through the Blake window. The Mother's halo was faintly illuminated, but her child's was alight. Blake must have designed the window so that dust didn't collect on the child's head.

The rest of the window itself was very dirty. I quickly got brushes and dusters to clean it. I cleaned the inside, then sat down facing the window. I stared at the outline of the Mother. She was naked. So was the Child on her knee. She looked down at me. The child looked up.

I felt profoundly calm. At the end of something good. At the start of something good. The window was alight. I was alight. I remember a tingling sensation all over my body, particularly at the back of my head and along my spine. Wave after wave of sensation throughout my brain and spine.

The window came nearer, the Mother—God the Mother—sitting solidly, compassionately over me, the Child absorbed in looking up. Both were listening to inner voices, kind of tuned in to the rhythm of their bodies and spirits.

The shadow of the east wing of the church began to move across the window. When the haloes darkened, I was suddenly empty. Disappointed. Deeply despondent. I had to be active.

I went out of the church and round to the window, and cleaned the outside thoroughly.

"What's this, then?" the policeman asked. I was carrying steps back into the church. He surprised me totally. I jerked round to look at him. He had a pocket radio in one hand and his pistol in the other. He spoke into his radio, keeping a curious eye on me.

"Good morning," I said when he clipped his radio away. He nodded, examining my face.

I continued into the church and he followed. He saw immediately that I'd been at work. I led him along to the Blake window and stood looking up at it.

"Are you alright, sir?"

"A bit staggered. That window came to life about an hour ago."

He glanced briefly up at the window, then again searchingly at my face. I moved around the church. He half-followed.

I said, "It must seem strange finding me here."

"It's not the strangest thing that's happened to me, but it did cross my mind that you are, perhaps, troubled . . . not quite all there."

"I'm staying with Mrs Johnson. I couldn't sleep."

His face changed expression rapidly. He nodded knowingly and put his pistol in his holster.

"I was in France recently and I met the last Rector. I . . ."

He was satisfied, I think, and looked as if he was about to leave. "I notice," I said, "you came in this church without taking off your hat and with your gun in your hand."

"Can't be too careful," he observed, wishing to be on his way.

"Churches mean nothing to you."

"Yes, churches do mean something to me . . ." he spoke heavily, ". . . pot-parties, pop-concerts, and official acid-scenes. Trouble in other words."

"Trouble is your business."

"Not quite, though you could put it like that. Protecting people from their own stupidities is how I would put it."

"Then you must be very busy."

"Too busy to hang around here at seven in the morning."

He seemed less interested in leaving. I got on with my work. He asked, "You say you met the last Rector. He's living with Mrs Johnson's daughter, isn't he?"

I nodded.

"Is there a child?"

I assented.

"A girl?"

"A boy."

"My wife told me about it. Mary Johnson drove him round the bend. It's not his kid."

He obviously had decided that I was a kind of simpleton. "What made you think it was a girl?"

"I wasn't here at the time but didn't she go round saying her child was the son of God?"

"It's a lovely thing to say," I suggested lamely.

"They're all God's kids but my missus told me that Mary Johnson's father got her pregnant."

I worked on. He added, "And that's why the Rector went crazy."

"He's not crazy now."

"Doesn't old man Johnson still live with them?"

"An unusual family."

He sat down and took off his hat. "You can say that again. I did psychology and sociology during my training, but I think the world's full of nutters." He looked up suddenly at me.

"I know the feeling," I said.

"High-faluting-nutters . . . explaining simple human mistakes in big words and psychology."

"You've got a simple explanation?"

"I've got a mouth, an arsehole and a cock. I breathe, I eat, I shit and I fuck. So does everybody else. I want my share. So does everybody else, so there's got to be control. What else is there?"

"No mystery? Nothing marvellous? Nothing lyrical?"

"Course there's a mystery. Will Leeds United win the European Cup. That's enough mystery for me. My kids, what will they be like . . . I suppose that's another. What will I be like when I'm old . . ."

"What about meaning?"

He mimed an erection with an expressive gesture of his right fore-arm, and clenched fist.

"You're lost," I told him.

"Lost or found, I don't have to come into churches in the early morning to look at windows and do the cleaning."

"Oh, I admit I'm lost. But I want to be found."

"Well, now, don't worry so much about it. I found you, didn't I?" He cracked out laughing. I remember feeling very foolish and frustrated. I looked across at the Blake window. Then I turned and stared up at the other window. I found it hard to distinguish the outline of the church inside the body of the woman.

"God, that church," Jane said as she cooked herself some breakfast. I asked, "Have you seen the window light up?"

"Never."

The bacon was crispy. The smell together with the sizzling and crackling in the pan made me want to eat. I asked her if she had any scales.

"In the bathroom," she said.

I came down.

"How much do you weigh?"

"Ninety-eight kilos."

"Are you sure you don't want breakfast?"

"Just coffee."

"Toast?"

"Just coffee."

"Sugar?"

She poured cream into the coffee.

"You want cream?"

I nodded, defeated slightly.

She put the cups and her plate on a tray and we went out onto the terrace to sit in the sun.

"Fantastic summer we're having," I said.

"When are you going to start work?"

"At the moment I haven't time to work."

She shrugged, eating quickly.

I went on, "There's a lot to do in the church, if you don't mind my staying here for a few days."

"That fucking church," she said through a mouthful of bacon.

"I'm surprised you haven't seen the window light up."

"My husband used to sleep in there so he wouldn't miss it."

"I can understand that."

"Then perhaps you can understand why I didn't want to see it."

"No, I can't."

"You think we should both have slept there?"

"Why not?"

"It would've made no difference. He, shall we say, neglected me in those days . . . now he wishes he . . ."

I cut in: "You sound very complacent."

She was angry, quivering slightly.

"That's one thing you can never say about me . . . nobody can ever say I'm complacent." She smoothed her hair with her right hand, forking bacon with her left.

I laughed aloud. She threw down her fork.

"Come on, Jane." I mimed: "There's one thing you can say about me . . . no-one can deny how complacent I am." I made to smooth down my hair and threw a fork onto the floor.

She smiled, mollified. She began to eat.

"Don't you need money?" she asked.

"Not at the moment."

"How long can you manage?"

"Perhaps a year . . . perhaps longer. I take in lodgers."

"Alistair told me about your lodger. It's a good thing my husband never thought of that when he was younger."

"You think of him as old?"

"Not really. He's always worked hard. That's one thing you can say about him. He worked bloody hard for his success."

"How did he live before?"

"He taught at the University."

"English?"

"Psychology."

"It wouldn't have surprised me if he'd taught theology."

"Psychology and Scepticism, he always used to say."

"Strange how religion comes into all his novels."

"He's a very religious man. The only trouble was that for him religion started between little girls' legs."

"Just little girls'?"

"Oh I think he was queer while he was up at Cambridge. They all were then."

"I meant, not up your legs."

"He was quite neurotic about sex with me. Once Mary was born, he went off it . . . at least he went off me. And the longer he was not having it with me, the more he wanted to go with little girls. I say little but I don't mean children. I mean young women. He was always open with them about it. And with me unfortunately. If I hadn't known about it maybe our life together might have been a bit better."

"Can you expect to live with a creative husband and live a normal life?"

"Don't give me that!" she said scornfully. "At first I thought it was just to hurt me. I still think that it sometimes was. But later I realised it was also a kind of terrible honesty . . . it was obviously to do with his guilt, but I think also it was honesty . . ."

"And you stayed with him."

"If I'd had a job . . . you know, something that really stretched me, I'm sure I'd 've left."

"As simple as that?"

She nodded. "We lived apart for much of each year."

"Did you . . . get around?"

She nodded again. "Not much. And he never knew about it. But I'm human. In fact, as you know, I'm very much a woman." She looked at me archly.

"I must get back to the church," I said.

"That fucking church," she replied, smiling. "You'll end up living in Beauvais."

"I hope so."

"You haven't drunk your coffee."

"You put too much cream in it."

That evening I video-telephoned the kids. They talked a little, were clearly alright, even Michael, but all three kept glancing towards where I assumed Margaret was standing. I asked to speak to her. Her face was flushed, excited. I told her I was thinking of going back to France for a while. She seemed to think it wasn't a bad idea. She told me I looked tired.

"I've been up since four this morning."

"You've started writing again."

"No. I was cleaning a church."

She stared from the screen.

"I'm alright," I said, "I went to see Seymore-Cartwright and he thinks I'm OK."

"What did you go to see him for?"

"Well . . . I wanted . . . you know, some kind of reassurance."

"Why didn't you come to me?"

"Perhaps I should've."

"What do you say you're doing? Cleaning a church?"

"You know the one . . . Mary Johnson's church."

"Is she there?"

"No . . . she's living in France."

"Who's there then?"

"Mary's mother."

Jane began to laugh. Someone else was standing near her. She turned to whoever it was and made a slight gesture.

"Is that David with you?"

Her face gave her away. She started to deny it was David. I flicked the video-phone off. I went into the sitting room. Jane was reading. I asked, "How are you feeling?"

My voice, the strain or something in it, made her look up.

"Are you alright?" she asked quickly.

"How are you feeling?" I asked again, taking the paper from her hand. Her dress was above her knees. I put my hand on her thigh. She looked into my face.

"Your face is a mask," she said.

"I want you."

She stiffened, resisting as my hand searched her thighs.

"I haven't washed," she said.

I began to undress her. She was still resistant when I began to kiss her belly and sex.

Afterwards she washed me. I was a child while she soaped, rinsed, dried and powdered me. I let her lead me to her bed.

She said, "When you came into the sitting room you treated me as an object."

"A desirable object." I was speaking like a sick man.

"Your wife upset you."

"She didn't mean to."

"Don't you believe it. If I could ever upset my husband, I always did . . . and I knew it."

"I feel quite weak."

"I'm not surprised. You've been fucking me for more than an hour."

"You were very good."

"Did I have a choice?" she asked.

There was a kind of acceptance-without-judgement, in the way she spoke. I began to cry.

She took off the dressing gown she was wearing and got into bed. Her body seemed older now, floppy about the waist, very creased, sagging in parts, firm in others. I wondered how I could have found her sexually attractive. When she rolled to me, she was just very warm. She put my head on her shoulder. I lay there awkward, crying still. I turned onto her tired breasts and shuddered, my shoulders heaving.

I woke up late the next morning. Jane came into the room carrying coffee and toast. She opened the curtains. The sun was dazzling. "Come on . . . you can't lie in my bed all day. It's nearly twelve o'clock." I sat up. She put the tray on my knees and went out, telling me not to be long.

I put the tray on the floor and lay back.

So Margaret and David were . . . what? Involved? I lay there trying to think of all the possibilities. I felt a mounting anger against David. Not anger, a kind of screeching, vicious and total aggression. I got up and dressed, determined to go home to see him. Kill him perhaps. I smiled. I glanced out and saw the church. I realised I'd missed seeing the window, and there was a lot of work still to be done. Undecided, I carried the tray downstairs.

"You haven't eaten anything," Jane said.

I sat down.

"Why," I asked, "would you upset your husband whenever you had the chance?"

"Oh, what I said last night? What I meant was that whenever I felt he'd upset me . . . well, the first chance I had I'd upset him. I was driven to it."

"But you loved him."

"Perhaps if you love someone you shouldn't marry them. I often feel that's where society is all wrong. I loved him so much that at times I wanted to murder him. I mean it. I don't think it's abnormal. He felt the same about me."

"Do you recognise yourself when he writes about you?"

"Yes. Sometimes I think that he's got me just right. Other times I think he's never understood me at all. Or himself."

"But it's not murder you mean . . . it's kind of killing all that's bad."

"With me it was murder. I've tried several times to murder him."

"Yes, but you'd try knowing he'd stop you."

She faltered a little. "Not always."

"If you'd wanted to kill him . . . really wanted to kill him, you'd have waited until he was asleep."

"But it wasn't when he was asleep that I wanted it."

"Exactly."

"What a terrible subject to be talking about."

"I must go and start work in the church."

"Will you tell your wife we've been lovers?"

"I don't need to. She'll assume we have. It will amuse her . . . someone older than herself."

"It'll still hurt her if I know women."

"Do you think so?"

"I know so."

David was very cocky. He moved about the café, cleaning the tables. I sat near the door. He kept looking across at me. Eventually, in his own time, he came over. "Want anything?"

"What were you doing at Margaret's?"

"I can go where I like, carn' I?"

He swaggered away.

"She's still my wife."

"I know. I respect that. You're my mate."

He went behind the counter. He looked across, his eyes cold, his mouth smiling:

"Neither Margaret nor me want to be possessive," he said.

"I don't want to be possessive either," I replied, "but . . ."

I remember putting my head in my hands.

"But what?"

"It's just the kids . . . what will the kids think?"

"I get on well with the kids . . . they're grand kids."

I was sickened. I retched, jerking the table away from in front of me. He stared across the counter. I glimpsed his set face as I retched again.

"Been eating something unpalatable?" he asked, his voice hard.

"I can deal with my own problems," I told him.

I wiped my mouth.

"Are you going to throw me out of your 'ouse?"

"You can stay there as long as you like. Keep out of my way."

I left without looking back.

Jill sat with me all the rest of that day. We played music but didn't speak much. Once or twice I began to touch her, but she didn't want to be touched.

"I've been to see David," I said eventually.

"He's lovely," she answered. "It's such a relief to know someone who's honest."

"David?"

She nodded.

"Does he want to sleep with you as well?"

She nodded.

"Have you?"

"Are you sure you should ask that question?"

"This is the end," I said.

"I know."

"I'm going to France anyway."

"I know."

"How?"

"David told me."

"How did he know?"

She shrugged her shoulders. "Margaret told him."

"All this malice."

"It isn't malice," she said calmly.

"It was good . . . between us."

"Not for me," she said.

"I'm sorry. You mean you never felt anything?"

"I love you," she said.

"I love you," I answered.

She turned away.

David came in the front door, hesitated outside the room Jill and I were in, then clumped upstairs. She asked: "Do you mind if I stay here for a little longer?"

"Not at all . . . stay here for as long as you wish."

She went out of the room.

I spent several days on my own. Jane Johnson telephoned a time or two, but I could barely speak to her. She understood, I think, and even worried about me enough to send Alistair over.

He came into the house, carrying several bottles of beer.

"How are you?" he asked. He didn't wait for a reply. He glanced around for glasses, then found his way into the kitchen, coming back with two mugs. He poured beer and handed me one of the mugs. He drained the other, filled it again, and sat down.

"Jane told you I was coming?"

I assented.

"She thinks you're upset."

"I am."

" 'Upset', she said."

"My sanity's beginning again."

He looked at me queerly. I said, "The last time I broke down I felt that it was the beginning of my sanity. Well, it's beginning again."

"It's guilt," he said.

"Shame more likely."

"Shame?"

"I found out how pathetically possessive I am."

" 'Possessive'," he repeated.

"What's wrong with you today? You're talking like a simpleton."

"I'm trying not to put a foot wrong."

"Look, I'm breaking through . . . I'm facing up to things."

"Well in that case, I may as well tell you what I think. I think you're a phony. I think you break down—Jane told me about your performance at her house—to get your own way."

"You too," I said.

"Just listen to the pious self-pity in your voice. You want me to think you're some kind of saint, delicate and tender, savaged by the insensitivities of those you love."

I was quiet.

"For my money," he said, "saints were business men, tough, unscrupulous, insensitive to others. Their commerce was ideas . . . freedom . . . love. When they were killed, and they always were and always will be, they stood up to it. No self-pity. Understanding, yes . . . that's different. Pain, yes, but they expected pain."

"Why are we talking about saints?"

"Just an example. You're far too soft with yourself."

"I do go in for self-pity. But it's bewildering."

"Do you expect it to be easy?"

"No. What are we talking about?"

He shrugged, laughed, drank his beer, put down the mug and stood up.

He said, "I'm hurt as well. *I*'ve got to give up things."

"What are we talking about?" I persisted.

He turned on me, angry: "I'm talking about going to live in France. It doesn't suit me . . ."

"You mean it doesn't suit Rachel."

"I like living with her."

"Won't she come with us?"

"No."

"You can commute."

"I want to live with her all the time."

"What will she do?"

"I suppose Donald will move in."

"I thought he might come to France as well."

"You don't know our Donald. He's a reactionary."

"I'd like to meet him."

"He doesn't meet people."

"Can you give her up?"

"I don't know. I hope so."

"When will you decide?"

"I think it's all decided, isn't it?"

We spent the day together. During the day I telephoned Christopher Arden-Jones at Beauvais. He told me the times of heli-planes landing at Beauvais and agreed to meet me.

Christopher collected me and noticed immediately that I was thinner.

"I'm down to ninety-six kilos," I said.

"It suits you. I'm glad you didn't forget us. We've talked about you a lot."

"I didn't want to leave."

"I know."

"You know that I made love to Mary."

"From what she told me, you made love to each other. You'll find we aren't fixated on sex. It may take you some time to get unhooked, if you see what I mean. But we've been unhooked for rather a long time. I say 'we', I mean I have. Mary's never seemed to have any problems, and of course the Boy will only learn about problems when he starts living outside our little group."

"You mean you aren't at all possessive?"

"I don't think I am. Maybe sometimes. I don't wish to be."

"If you happen to see Mary and some other . . ."

"She's not promiscuous, you know. She's beautiful. I think I was happy when she came to your room. We both knew how agitated you were. It was good to know she was there."

"I gave *her* something."

"Sure," he said.

I felt immediately sorry.

"Oh . . . I didn't mean to say that . . ."

"That's perfectly all right, Tony. We've all been looking forward to your coming. I'm delighted you've got here."

I was mystified but already had enough to think about.

Mary took me to the same room as before. I said, "I seem to be making progress." She waited. I went on, "I've been kind of liberated through sex."

"It's been liberating for you," she said, "but was it liberating for your partners?"

"You were one of them."

She looked at me gracefully.

"Every time I make love I feel freer. It's a beautiful, dark mystery."

"The last remaining mystery," I said.

"Oh no, Tony, not at all . . . the only one that twentieth-century man admits, perhaps. And the one he has to get through to reach other mysteries . . ."

"Get through?"

She smiled, looking into my face. I asked: "Is that what I'm doing?"

She spoke ironically, laughing lightly: "Ah yes . . . sex, the royal road to that country where men can love what they have learned to fear and hate in themselves . . ."

She sat down on the bed.

Silence.

"Thank God there is a way through," I said eventually.

"For everyone who puts his hand through to take it."

"It was easy for you," I said.

"It's never easy."

"Sorry, I understand that . . . but why did you do it when so few even try?"

"Parents . . . my father mostly, I think . . . he was brother, son . . . most things a male can be to a female. He also could be female when he tried really hard, or rather, when he didn't try . . . a sister . . . mother. You know he brought me up? Jane worked." She paused, "So that he's been as complete a person to me as . . . well, as anyone could dream of."

"That sounds very precious."

"It would've been precious, ghastly, if his motives had been at all sadistic or masochistic. But he is a true lover."

"He must have had a marvellous mother."

"That's right. And a marvellous wife."

"She is good, isn't she," I said.

"She tells me you've been working in the church."

"I've cleaned it."

"You saw the window."

I didn't have to answer. Mary listened to her inner voices. I sat down, thinking about the window. I began to be excited. Mary looked at me. I observed, "Christopher said that you were looking forward to my coming back."

"We knew you would want to. And we got messages from England about you . . . from Jane of course, and from Peter Seymore-Cartwright. And we meet so few honest people, it's exciting finding one."

"But I'm not honest."

"Exactly."

I told her about David, about my wife, Jill. She listened interested, without comment.

I rested in the early evening and was woken up by the sound of several piston-driven cars, without exhausts, being blasted at speed around the house. I looked out of the window to see Anthony Johnson appear with a shot-gun, followed by Christopher carrying another. The cars rounded the house again, bursting through fences and over vegetables and flowers. Mary joined her father. I put on trousers and rushed out. Anthony said. "There's a ·22 in the umbrella stand in the hall." I went and got the gun. The Boy followed me out.

The next time the cars came roaring round they stopped, facing us. There were three or four wild youngsters in each car. It was hard to distinguish male from female. They sat looking at us, laughing, making fun, drinking from litre-bottles of whisky.

I counted. Thirteen. I checked the firing mechanism of the ·22. Anthony looked around and indicated that Christopher and I should move apart. The biggest car was open, without bonnet, wings, windows. In the back, slumped well down in his seat, was a man of about twenty-five, different from the others. He was cleanly-shaven, wore the white shirt and dark suit of a bank-clerk, and balanced an automatic rifle in both hands.

The three of us, armed, against thirteen of them. Mary and the Boy in the background. The bank-clerk spoke to the others—none of their cars had windows—and they cracked out laughing again. He looked across at us, and stood up on the seat. The others got out of their cars. All had guns. They were now serious.

The bank-clerk called out, speaking good English. "You, the old man in the middle, you playing John Wayne in this piece?"

"What do you want?" Anthony asked.

"Money, drink and fun."

"Do you want to die to get it?" Anthony asked.

"Why not," the bank-clerk replied.

Mary walked towards them. She indicated the chickens and turkeys they had strewn about their cars. "You've got meat. We have vegetables . . ." "You're a beautiful mother," the bank-clerk interrupted. "Isn't she, boys and girls?" Mary continued, "We can make a fire out here in the open and cook the birds."

Silence. The Boy walked towards them. He was naked. They seemed to recognise him.

"Why not?" the bank-clerk said. "Put down your guns, boys and girls."

Anthony and I didn't trust them, and stood holding our guns long after they had joined in the building of two huge fires. They ignored us, as did Mary, the Boy and Christopher.

"What do you think?" I called across to Anthony.

"They're making monkeys out of us," he said. "I'll go and get some wine."

He laid down his gun carefully, checking the safety-catch, and went into the house.

It was almost dark when the food was ready. Already much drinking had been done. Two of the girls, their shirts open to the waist, passed a litre-bottle of wine to each other as they sweated with Mary over the fires. Anthony and the bank-clerk were talking seriously to each other. Anthony's face was very alive. He looked a young man. Christopher and I were sitting uncertainly among the gang.

I noticed Anthony was drinking little. The bank-clerk, as he emphasised something to Anthony, suddenly noticed Mary working over the fire. She stopped work to wipe her forehead with the back of her wrist. Then she took off her cardigan and unfastened the neck of her blouse. She became aware of the bank-clerk. They looked at each other, then she turned back to her work.

Anthony said to him, "Where did you do your degree in sociology?"

The bank-clerk smiled, nodding appreciatively. "Good thinking, old man. You the celebrated writer?"

"Your father's wealthy, you've got tired of his women, everything means nothing to you . . ." The bank-clerk was smiling, still nodding. Anthony added, ". . . and you spend too much time watching old movies."

The bank-clerk looked around at his group. "The celebrated writer knows what it's all about." He turned back to Anthony, "Do you know everything about me, old man?"

Anthony shook his head. Mary came over carrying roasted chickens. With her hands she broke off legs and passed them around. The bank-clerk persisted with Anthony, "Can you finish the picture?"

"You're very confident," Anthony said, "so I take it there are more of you out there." He gestured into the night. "Perhaps you're about twenty or so. Your group changes because kids today get tired of playing movies. But you don't. One of them will eventually see the payoff for talking about you. You get cornered, your group leave you and you're faced with the choice of being taken or killed. Either way you get headlines. You prefer to be taken, so you can enjoy a gorgeous trial."

"Not bad, old man."

"But you've left out your father. That's always been your mistake. You forget that he's still in there. He decides there isn't gonna be a trial. So you offer to give yourself up but your offer is refused."

"So the old man wins."

"Do you want to eat?" Mary asked the bank-clerk.

Anthony, looking intently into the bank-clerk's face, said, "Why not?"

"I'd like to eat your tits," the bank-clerk said to Mary.

I moved to Mary's side.

The bank clerk asked Anthony, "Who's the nervy one?", meaning me.

Christopher came over and stood with me.

Anthony said, "I'll tell you his story if you're here in the morning."

Mary accepted the attentions of the bank-clerk, touching my arm to reassure me and glancing easily at Christopher who also, I guessed, needed some kind of reassurance. I went and sat near Anthony, asking him what he thought.

"They might want to kill us but I doubt it," he said quietly.

"Why should they?"

"Didn't you hear what they wanted? Money, drink and fun." He emphasised 'fun'.

Two of the youngest—both about fifteen, maybe fourteen—sat with the Boy who ate heartily, taking an occasional mouthful of wine when they passed him their bottle. He asked them questions and they answered him, their behaviour thoughtful, passionate once or twice, unsatisfying for them. They became quiet. The Boy took their hands.

An older youth, I think a girl, came over and began to make fun of the Boy's nakedness. He looked up at her, trying to understand what she felt. She sat down and, brushing aside the two younger ones, mimed cuddling him, then kissing his body. The others laughed, uneasily. She touched his sex several times and then bent towards it. He was erect.

I caught Christopher's attention, then Anthony's. The bank-clerk saw what was happening. He said, "Le petit Jésus?" He laughed. Then he picked up his rifle, cocked it, and pointed it at Anthony. The girl went down properly to the Boy who leaned back, watching her. His face suddenly clouded, and he searched round for Mary. When their eyes met, he stared at her, his face troubled, confused. He leaned forward, putting both hands gently on the head of the sucking girl. His body became tense. Her movements became frenzied. Then stopped.

Everybody was tense. The bank-clerk clearly wanted to defend the girl, expecting Anthony and Christopher—he even included me in his watchful, taunting stare—to do something to her. Mary stood up and walked over to the Boy. She lightly touched his head with both hands, then she turned her attention to the crouching, breathless girl. Mary raised the girl to her feet. The girl kept her face away from Mary. The girl's hair was over her eyes. Mary very gently persuaded the girl to look up, delicately fingering the hair from her eyes. They looked at each other. Mary was relaxed, reassuring. The girl held her head up, staring into

Mary's eyes. Asserting something deep within her. Mary encouraged the girl's mouth to her own. They kissed lightly.

"I needed to kiss you," Mary murmured to the girl.

Later, the bank-clerk sent out some of his group and others came in. They were sober, almost respectable. Among them was a man of about twenty-two who sat next to the bank-clerk and immediately began to explain the dangers of staying there.

Apart from a couple having sex, there was little activity. Mary and the Boy sat together and eventually went into the house to sleep. Christopher asked the bank-clerk if they wished to stay the night, and when the bank-clerk shook his head, offered his hand. Then Christopher went in. Suddenly the group stood up. The bank-clerk looked at Anthony.

"Money?" Anthony asked.

"Correct, old man," answered the bank-clerk.

Anthony went into the house and came out with nearly four hundred pounds in English and French money. He looked at me. I produced another hundred pounds or so. Anthony said, "To save you time, that's all there is."

The bank-clerk accepted the money, handing it to his twenty-two year-old colleague, and then looked at Anthony.

"Drink?" Anthony said.

The bank clerk nodded. I went in with Anthony. He had two cases of whisky in his cellar and many bottles of wine. We lugged the whisky up to the waiting gang.

"Thanks," said the bank-clerk. "We came a long way to see what your group is like, old man."

They faced each other.

"When you can tell me my story," Anthony said, "come back, if they let you get here."

"We'd better go," said his colleague.

They got in their cars except for the bank-clerk. He stood, still reluctant to leave Anthony. Eventually, as the engines exploded, the bank-clerk asked:

"Will I be able to make it?"

"Come back here with your father some day," Anthony said quietly.

"I never knew my old man, old man, but you're still on the right track."

"I kept saying 'come back' because I wanted to feed him the idea that we had to be here to come back to," said Anthony when the noise of their engines faded.

"You were good," I said.

"I was fairly good, I had everything going for me."

"You mean . . ."

"His insecurities. The tremendous personas of Mary and the kid. But I got it wrong."

We sat without speaking in front of the low fires. Mary came out and sat with us. She touched Anthony's foot. "You did well," she said.

He looked into her face, smiling.

She went on, "When they put your guns into one of the cars, I thought . . ."

I was surprised and glanced to where my rifle had been.

"They really could've killed us," I said nervously.

"It's a bit too soon for that," Anthony said, and burst into laughter. Mary smiled broadly.

"Should we stay here?" I asked.

"Good question, soldier," Anthony said with a John Wayne accent, "we'll break camp in the morning."

Mary and I saluted him as he went in.

"Good night," she said and followed.

I lay on my back, recognising the stars, naming them and searching for their neighbours. Listening also for the sound of piston-cars.

The next morning in a fine burst of energy, Anthony organised a visit south to the pre-historic cave-dwellings at Les Eysies in the

Dordogne. He hired a heli-taxi and we arrived in the late afternoon. On the way down, he asked me to think about taking the Boy to England pretty well straight away.

We stayed in a large hotel in Le Bugue, a few miles from the caves. I must admit that my interest was in being with Mary's family, and it wasn't until we arrived at Les Eysies and saw the chalk-cliff, with its caves that I began to think about pre-historic man. Then again, when Christopher, the Boy and I went into one of the caves, leaving Anthony and Mary to go round museums, I was far more interested in the Boy's reactions. He went about touching, smelling, looking, listening to the interior. He leaned his head and arms on the worn parts, seemingly alert to any vibrations or traces left behind by the pre-historic occupiers.

Then we came to some drawings. The first was a bison. The outline was austerely, accurately drawn. The contours of the wall had been chosen exactly to give the third dimension, so that we were looking at an animal that existed. And it had existed for many thousands of years. Yet the man who had drawn and coloured the bison was supposed to be primitive, pre-historic. The Boy sat down in front of the beast looking up at it, keen that the guide should explain how the colour was made. I stared at the bison trying to understand why it was so completely impressive. The animal was there. It was so successfully represented that one knew it was no special beast, merely one of the millions that through endless time had breathed, eaten, excreted, reproduced and died. He was magnificently ordinary. Yet substantial and somehow perfect. I remembered Anthony saying to the Boy, the first time I arrived at Beauvais, that all good art throughout time makes the same statement.

The Boy traced the outline of the bison. He was absorbed. After the first few minutes of revelation, I became bored and I went out of the cave, leaving Christopher and the Boy. It was good to get into the fresh green valley again.

That evening I watched them eat paté truffé, truite à l'aile, confit de canard—with Anthony and Christopher enthusing over each mouthful—cheese, followed by crêpes flambées. Anthony chose dishes and wines with an authority and gusto that I envied.

After dinner, Mary, the Boy and Christopher went for a walk they'd planned. Anthony led me out onto the terrace overlooking the smelly river. The swallows darted about high in the sky, occasionally swooping down to their nests under a ledge in the old stone bridge. Fish were rising steadily in the fast-running water.

Anthony smoked a cigar, spitting on the terrace occasionally. "It's clean spit," he explained, "I hate the taste of these bloody cigars but I like making the gestures of smoking them."

We sat, silent.

"I've read your books," I said.

"They stand up, don't they?"

"You kind of conceived Mary in them."

"The people who live in my books create themselves."

I persisted, "But you're interested in fathers and daughters a lot."

"Sons and mothers as well. Whoever's in my pieces got in there under his own steam."

"So Mary's become one of the daughters in one of your novels?"

"Listen, don't underestimate Mary . . . or Jane . . . or any of my family. We're in big business . . ." He hesitated, smiling strangely, tensing forward on his chair to study the river ostentatiously. ". . . I think we've made it. We're just about to go public. That's why you're here."

"I don't understand."

He guffawed, leaning back, holding his belly. I remember feeling angry. "Look." He spluttered a little. "Will you allow me to show you something?" I was reserved, trying to work out in what way I was being abused. He explained, "We've got things to talk about, you and me. In which case I'd like to show you a grand lady. She's seven thousand years old." He got up, assuming that I wanted to go.

He drove to Les Eysies and parked near the centre of the village. People were wandering about in the quiet soft air.

As we walked he tried to describe how the people in his books got into them without any efforts from him. "My integrity as a writer—such as it is, and while I think I have integrity, each reader decides for himself—depended on my not being there in the novel. I put no linking passages, no little descriptions, demonstrating the writer's virtuosity, sensitivity and wisdom, nothing. I wait at my typewriter and when they talk and do things, I get it down. Without comment. I am like a secretary. The servant of the characters."

"But you're merely saying you do it unconsciously."

"Maybe. But the people have all lived before. I found myself writing up-to-date versions of the oldest story in the world. The mental traveller. The guy who descends into hell to get wisdom; ascends into heaven, then returns, usually with a young girl who becomes the mother of the next generation of more-knowing travellers. You know, like James Bond. In a sick way, Bond is Jesus."

"But his women always get killed."

"Exactly . . . that's the sickness."

Above us loomed a larger-than-life statue of prehistoric man, L'Homme de Cromagnon, his ponderous head turned, looking upwards at the darkening sky. Anthony looked up. I said, "He's not what you wanted to show me?"

He shook his head. "They used to rear humans as slaves until they were old enough to be eaten. Imagine, you fuck whichever slave-girl you fancy, then you eat her and rear her kids. Maybe your woman does the killing and the cooking." I gazed up at the brutal flanks and shoulders of the stone-age man until my neck ached. "Come and look at this," Anthony said, leading me into the museum. The keeper knew him well, and they talked intimately about recent finds in one of the caves. Again, I envied Anthony's knowledge and gusto. He took the keeper, who I gathered was a student doing his Ph.D. in Anthropology, to demonstrate what he was saying by showing him the details on a group of little human figures kept in a glass case. The keeper unlocked the case and they went into a precise conversation, Anthony talking volubly, the keeper listening, his face grave. I wandered around glancing here and there until I suddenly came across the statue of a woman. She was formidable. 'Venus de Laussel circa five thousand BC.' She was real. Looking at me. Huge breasts, heavy with milk and with touching, tasting implications. Strong, gross thighs, leading to her sex which was prominent, sturdily open to be entered.

"You found her," Anthony said.

"God the fecund Mother."

"To be fucked endlessly and forever," he added, crossing himself and genuflecting.

"At least." We both laughed.

"Does she remind you of anybody?" he asked as we walked away. I think he wanted me to 'find' her in his novels. "All the women who've shared their bodies with me," I said.

We were passing under L'Homme de Cromagnon. "Do you know what you're doing?" Anthony asked, his voice somehow careful.

I didn't understand what he was asking. "I'm walking with a well-known writer, in the south-west of France . . ."

He cut in, "I mean, you fuck my wife. You fuck my daughter. You instal yourself in my house."

I can't remember what I mumbled. I think, in my confusion, I apologised, but Anthony wasn't interested. He suddenly slapped me on the back, took my arm to direct me to where his hired car was parked, and, looking closely into my face, he observed proudly, "That wasn't a bad question."

"My wife thinks I'm crazy . . . destroying myself."

"And what do you think?"

"I think," I said, pausing, not at all sure of what I did think, "I think . . . maybe I'm becoming a character in one of your novels."

He started the electric engine. "I think I want to fart," he said. Mechanically, I pressed the switch that opened the windows. He laughed at me so much that for a time I had to lean over and hold the steering-wheel, my head almost on his shoulder as I avoided the oncoming traffic.

Mary and I sat in the hotel lounge after the others had gone to bed. Plucking up courage I asked, "Do you think that the theme of your father's novels was too huge for him?"

"Which theme?" she asked.

"Men producing gods. He was really trying to re-write the New Testament."

"I don't think like that. He wrote about people."

"But things happen to them that don't happen in real life."

"What you think is real is only the cover. And he was writing fiction."

What are you covering, I thought, my mind suddenly active. "But it's not as simple as that. You're part of the fiction. Do you mind my saying that you aren't real?"

"Am I real with you?"

I remembered our sex . . . everything she was to me. "Yes, but there are no shadows to you . . . didn't you once say you had no unconscious?"

"I meant that I don't find myself repressing or inhibiting my experience."

"But that's silly, isn't it? Everybody has to do that. Humans have to do it."

She smiled warmly. "Having an unconscious is silly, surely. Having knowledge, acting on it, yet not knowing you have it."

"I don't understand."

"Why are you involving yourself with me and my son?"

Of course I didn't know why. I remember being irritated at this point. But I sensed that there was something she could tell me so I persisted: "I vaguely know that I have to, but not why. Can you tell me?"

"I'm afraid not."

"Not?" I was flabbergasted. "I've come here to fulfil some kind of calling and you don't know what it is?"

"I don't wish to tell another person what his calling is."

"But don't I get any . . ." She waited for me to find the right word. I thought of 'instruction', then 'teaching', then 'special knowledge'. ". . . help?" I said eventually.

"Oh, we'd like to help you. And we're delighted you've come to live with us."

"There you are," I protested, "you said 'come to live'. I didn't know I had."

"Who knows how long you'll stay?"

"But you expected me."

"I expect there'll be others."

"But won't you do anything about it until they come?"

"Not even then."

"You'll have to get a larger house."

"Why do you say that?"

"There'll be twelve of us, won't there?"

"You're taking it all far too seriously," she said, leaning forward to kiss me lightly on the lips.

We went to more caves on the second and third days. We talked of driving leisurely back to Beauvais, but there were political demonstrations in and around Paris that might have become unpleasant, so Anthony insisted on our going back by heli-taxi.

The feeling I had at this time was that the Boy was staying away from me. In the heli-taxi we sat together. I told him that I thought he didn't find me very interesting.

"You are a bit boring," he said.

"You mean I'm always asking questions."

"Not only that. You think of me as special."

"But you are different."

"What are your children like?"

"Well, they've got names, for a start."

"Did they choose their names?"

"No."

"If ever I choose a name, I'll probably choose several, or a different one every day."

"I think they'd find it confusing not to have a name."

"It is when you meet people who don't know you."

"What happens?"

"I tell them I haven't a name."

"Then what happens?"

"Oh, sometimes we get talking."

"Do you meet many people?"

"You're asking questions," he said, smiling. All the time he talked he seemed to be both listening and thinking.

"As if you're special," I said, catching the drift of his thought.

"Yes."

"Well, it seems as if we're going to find it very hard to have a conversation ever again."

"Why should we have conversations?"

"I would like to get to know you."

"Do we have to have conversations for that?"

"I suppose what I ought to say is I'd like to get to unknow you."

"That's what I try and do," he said.

"You're quite right, I do think of you as special. Perhaps we should do something together."

"I'm interested in schools," he said.

Back in Beauvais, Anthony and Mary thought it was a good idea for the Boy to go to England with me so I could show him round English schools. He was very keen, and Christopher, who wanted to see Jane Johnson, thought he would come with us. I asked Mary and Anthony to come also, implying there was danger in staying where they were. Neither seemed to agree. Both had things to do which required them to stay on at least for a week or two.

That evening we were visited by an attractive, very chic young woman, who entered the house apprehensively. Mary and the Boy immediately recognised her. I was slower. The Boy held out his hand, easing slightly away from her at the same time as if unwilling to impose. She was unwilling to accept his hand, but equally unwilling to refuse it. She stood, indecisive, until Mary went over to her and took her hand as well as the Boy's. Speaking French, Mary welcomed her, asked her name—Anne-Marie—and offered her food. Anne-Marie looked from Mary's face to the Boy's. She appeared to be deeply moved, as if in an emotional crisis.

Anthony, somewhat roughly, invited Christopher and me into the dining room. He closed the doors on the three while Christopher opened a bottle of wine. We drank ruminatively.

"Who is Anne-Marie?" I asked.

Anthony and Christopher exchanged glances. Anthony said, "The Boy's girlfriend."

I was puzzled. She looked to be eighteen or even older.

They're treating me as an outsider, I thought. I felt niggled, then angry. Christopher turned to look at me. I spoke angrily, standing up to hand my glass to Christopher so that he could fill it: "I'm out of it in such serene company."

"Don't be an arsehole," Anthony said evenly.

Christopher carefully filled my glass, checking that none of the sediment got into it. He handed the glass back with a quiet smile. "She's the piston-gang-girl who had sex with the Boy."

Anthony glanced at Christopher, then at me. I felt foolish. "It's difficult coming among you," I said, "particularly as I don't know what's going on."

Anthony asked me if I'd expected it to be easy.

"No, but I wish someone'd tell me what I'm getting involved in."

"He who knows, doesn't say," Anthony said, sounding like a Chinese sage. Christopher added, "It's more a question of doing things than knowing them, though I know how awfully frustrating it must be for you to hear such comments."

You don't know, I thought. "I'm sorry," I said, "I'm the kind of person who needs words."

Neither felt he had to offer me any more that evening.

Christopher travelled to England with the Boy and me, leaving us at Leeds to go on to Jane Johnson's. I took the Boy home, very unsure of how he would adapt to my way of living. I was keen to introduce him to my kids, to Alistair, even to David and Jill. But underneath my keenness was a sense of bewildering involvement with the process that was taking me along, like a river in which I was just managing to keep my head above water.

My youngest son, John, came round to see me at about eight that evening. He'd heard his mother say I was back. I explained to the Boy who John was, then said to John:

"This is a friend of mine from France, he hasn't got a name."

John looked at me, sharply curious. The Boy said, "Children in England have names."

"Do you want to see the room I used to have?" John asked, and ran up the stairs, the Boy following.

I didn't see them for about two hours.

Later, my wife video-phoned to ask if John was still with me.

"Yes, How are you?"

"I'm rotten if you want to know."

Silence. I said, "I daren't ask you if you're having your period."

"Well, I am. But it's nothing to do with that. I'm having my heads again. I hate my work. I'm tired of all the pathetic males in this town lining up at my door thinking I'm an easy lay. Christopher is too big to share a room with John. And I'm short of money."

Silence.

'Well," she demanded, "what are you going to do about it?"

"I'm not going to rush round with a cheque-book."

"I didn't think you would. I don't know why you bother to ask."

"I can try to understand . . . offer a bit of support."

She snorted, her voice rising to a scream:

"Ugh. How dare you offer to support me. What makes you think you can? I've got all the worry . . . all the responsibilities . . . you go off to France on some crazy dream to fuck the holy virgin while I struggle with the kids' homework. I get no time for any life of my own . . . I'm fed up. I think you ought to have them for a few weeks."

"Look, I'll bring John up and we can have a talk."

"What about?"

"Come on, Margaret, we love each other."

"That's a damn lie for a start. What do you think I want to talk about with you?"

"I'd like to see you."

"Are you on your own?"

"I've got a Boy with me."

"A what?"

"I'll bring him up with John."

She was bristling with aggressive and suggestive questions, so I switched off.

John and the Boy appeared about twenty minutes later. John was holding his hand and leading him to me, clearly wanting to ask a question. I guessed, "You want to know who chose your name."

John smiled and nodded.

"Ask mummy. I can't remember, but it might have been me."

"Can I change it if I want to?"

"You'd better talk with mummy first."

I asked the Boy if he was hungry. He shook his head.

"My wife is rather upset and I'd like to take John home and see her."

"Can I come?" he asked.

I hesitated. "Of course. But she's very angry."

"With you?" he asked.

John said, "Of course it's with dad . . . she's always angry with him. She left him."

"My wife and I stopped living with each other about four months ago."

"Do many people stop living together?"

John said, "Lots."

"And it makes them angry with each other?" he asked.

"Mummy and Daddy," said John, "have always been angry with each other."

I was upset at this. John noticed.

"Not all the time," he added, "but lots of it. Come on, I'll show you my soldiers."

At Margaret's John took the Boy upstairs to the room he shared with Christopher. Margaret was sitting in her lounge. Annie—my daughter—popped her head out of the dining room and asked if I wanted coffee. I nodded, adding, "There's a friend of mine, a Boy, up with John. Do you want to say hello?"

"Not if he's like John." she said. "Still not taking sugar?"

I nodded.

"I might go up," she said, going into the kitchen.

I went cautiously in to see Margaret.

"Who's this boy?"

"He's Mary Johnson's son."

She stared at me.

"Jesus?"

"He hasn't chosen a name yet."

"You mean she's not given him a name."

"Listen, I want you to meet him. He's a very unusual child."

"She let him come to England with you!"

"She wants him to be free."

"Hum . . . then she must've got herself a good husband who accepts his responsibilities. I suppose she's fallen for you."

"She's not the kind of person to fall."

"Does John get on with him?"

"Absolutely naturally."

"What do you call him if he hasn't a name?"

"It's embarrassing for a bit."

She glanced at the clock.

"Look at the time . . . it's nearly half past ten. I'm having terrible trouble with John, getting him off to sleep. What do you mean by keeping him out till now?" Her voice was weakening as she spoke, the conviction disappearing. We talked for nearly an hour. At first she was bitter and full of accusations. After a while I got her talking about the advantages of living on her own, and she became more relaxed.

My coffee never appeared and eventually I offered to make her a cup. She followed me into the kitchen, still talking. There was a mug of coffee, quite cold.

I put on water and went into the dining room. Annie and the Boy were talking intimately. Annie looked up and smiled,

"I l. . .l. . .like your friend, Dad. Isn't it funny he hasn't a name?"

"Well, it's unusual," I said, looking at his relaxed face.

"And he hasn't got a mother and a father either," she said. Margaret came into the room and the Boy stood up.

"This is my wife . . . Margaret, a friend of mine from France."

Margaret held out her hand and he took it very seriously.

"Tony said you were angry," he commented.

"I was," she said.

"He hasn't got a father or mother," Annie said.

"Oh, dear, that's terrible," Margaret answered, looking at me for enlightenment.

Annie said, "Oh, I don't think so. It sounds lovely . . . no quarrels."

"Your father and I aren't always quarrelling."

"No, but you don't get on. I'd love to have no parents."

Margaret was upset.

"I'd love to have some for a few days, just to see," the Boy said.

Margaret looked at him gratefully. Then to Annie:

"You'd soon change your tune, my girl, if I wasn't here."

The Boy was very alert, watching the exchange, anxious for it in some kind of way.

"Where's John?" Margaret asked.

"I put him to bed," the Boy said, "he was tired."

"Did he fall asleep?" she asked, surprised.

"I told him a story and he just dropped off."

She turned to me: "There you are. If you were here facing up to your responsibilities, I'd have time to tell him stories."

"Do you feel," the Boy asked Margaret, "that you know what responsibilities other people have?"

She stared at him, surprised, on her guard, feeling in danger—I think this is how she felt—of being exposed in some way.

"When children have got a father and mother," she said slowly, "in this country, we all know what their responsibilities are. Everybody agrees."

He turned to me, wanting me to comment.

"Margaret thinks she knows what my responsibilities are, but I don't agree with her."

"Everybody I've talked to agrees with me," Margaret said firmly.

"But it could be," he said, "that they say what you want to hear. Or it could be you only ask those who'll agree with you."

"Yes, mum," Annie said, "I think that. Your friends all do agree with you but I...I...I bet they don't behind your back."

"Or maybe they do," I said quickly.

Margaret looked at the Boy. He moved towards her, his face expressing real concern. She said, "What does your mother think about my husband?"

He thought about her question. I heard the water boiling in the kitchen. I looked at Annie but she shook her head, she wanted to hear his answer.

"She thinks that he's an honest man. We all do. We want him to live with us."

"But what about his kids? Do you want them to come and live with you?"

"I can only speak for myself. I would be delighted," he answered.

"So would I," Margaret said heavily.

"You're saying that because you feel unsure of yourself," the Boy said.

"I've never felt surer," Margaret insisted, half-looking at Annie.

Annie's eyes were filling.

"You'd never let them go," I said to Margaret warmly.

Annie went out to the kitchen.

Margaret sat down suddenly. The Boy went over and put his hand on her head. She feebly tried to shrug it off, but then she leaned to him and he put both arms round her. She began to cry heavily.

I went out and left them. Annie was crying also. I took her in my arms. I said, smiling, "I'm holding you in my arms and the Boy's holding mummy in his."

"Mummy's terrible when she says things like that."

"But, Annie, you know it's because she's tired and she's having her period."

"I know it's partly that," she said quickly, "but she's at John all the time now. It worries me."

"It seems bad to you, but it'll all work out. We all love each other. You see, everything 'll slowly work out."

"It's easy for you to say that," she said, touching my face gently, "you're doing what you want . . . you're free. Mummy's got us."

"I would like to have you as well. Perhaps you think we should all live together again."

"No, I didn't mean that. It's just that I worry about John. He's only eight."

"It wouldn't help if I said that I think he'll be alright?"

"No, it wouldn't," she said, wiping her tears from her eyes. "What time is it?"

"Nearly midnight."

"I'd better go to bed. Goodnight."

She kissed me quickly. I hugged her until she gently pushed me away and went upstairs.

Margaret and the Boy were talking quietly. I heard their voices as I went up to kiss Annie goodnight again and to pop in to John. He was sound asleep.

It was nearly one o'clock before Margaret, enormously pleased with herself, came into the sitting room.

"Quite a boy . . . he's grown up really," she said.

"I'm tired."

She kissed me goodnight.

Walking down to my house, I said, "She's a very good girl."

"She's stiff down to her bottom," he replied.

"You mean the bottom of her personality."

He nodded: "And her body. Her fingers are stiff, her limbs, her words."

"She's usually constipated as well," I said impulsively, half-laughing. He went on seriously.

"She wants you to make her unstiff . . . if not you, then somebody else. She doesn't think she should try and do it herself."

"Did she bore you?"

"She's the first woman in sin I've listened to."

"In sin?"

"She talks of love as a sort of duty. She makes herself love and expects to have to make others love her."

"But underneath all that she's warm and spontaneously lovely."

"I believe she is," he agreed.

There was a problem over where the Boy should sleep. I offered him my bed with the idea of my sleeping downstairs, but he didn't understand why we shouldn't sleep in the same bed. Nor did I.

The next morning I found a note from David, with a postscript by Jill, both welcoming me home. I spent the morning making arrangements for the Boy to visit several schools the next day and dealing with the pile of letters, several from Margaret's lawyers, that either David or Jill had piled in chronological order on the floor of the still-empty hall. I didn't see the Boy till lunch-time when he went into the kitchen to make an omelette with some of the eggs that David habitually stole from the café—his perks, he called them. We ate in the breakfast room. I asked him what he thought about my kids.

"I like to meet children. They can be more interesting than adults," he said, smiling.

That afternoon, after getting the Boy some warm clothes which he felt were unnecessary, we wandered into the cathedral. He noticed immediately that there were none of the statues and religious pictures one finds in churches in France. He searched around and turned to look at me. "No mother," he said, delighted.

"It's a Protestant cathedral," I pointed out. "Do you like churches?"

"I'm interested in what they say."

He wandered about, looking up continually at the gothic arches and the carved angels holding up the roof.

In the cloisters we found ourselves moving among a group of dreamy-eyed people. I recognised several psychologists and psychiatrists from our local hospital, a parson or two, several women-teachers, about half of the cathedral-clergy, and a sprinkling of young people. The Boy looked at me questioningly. I explained that this was one of the supervised LSD sessions for which the Cathedral was well-known. Twice I'd seen this group on television. In spite of the attentions of the TV cameras, with its aftermath—aftermyth?—the group had lived on. The behaviour of the group-members reminded me of the Boy's in the cave at Les Eysies. Several were touching the medieval stone-work of the cloisters, using not only the skin of their bodies and limbs, but also their mouths and tongues. Others were sitting or lying on the worn stone-flags. Two couples, one of a woman and a girl, the other of a priest and a young man, were touching each other. The supervisor—one of the young general practitioners of the town—was interested in the reactions of the Boy who was immediately in tune with the group, and initially, they with him. The Boy's rapport with the group caused him to become its focus. He stood among them, looking into their faces, touching each in turn.

The supervisor was kind of pleased. He asked me about the Boy. I told him as little as possible.

"He's a natural," he said. "Would you like a trip?"

"I had one once. It was bad. Very bad."

"Where did you have it?"

"In a psychiatric hospital."

"That's the last place to take acid. Bad trips come from a bad scene."

"Never from a bad psyche?"

"I suppose there are some people who ought not to use it. But it's pretty easy to recognise them and keep them out of a group."

"I'm one of those," I said definitively.

He looked at me and shrugged. "I would've thought the opposite," he said.

He wandered among the group towards a woman who was beginning to cry. I sat down, glancing around at the stonework. I liked (and still like) this cathedral. I knew most of the gargoyles and often, when I couldn't sleep, thought about them, particularly those in the cloisters, which, unlike those on the outside of the building, had scarcely weathered and remained the profane shapes the masons had in mind when they carved them in the late fourteenth century. I have a technique which I use in churches, of letting my eyes go out of focus and emptying my mind. Time seems to melt and I see things. On this occasion I saw all the gargoyles at once, each in the many stages of being carved. I heard the sounds of chisels and human voices, human smells intermingling with the noises and the shapes. Noises became shapes, shapes became smells, smells became colours. Or rather, noises, shapes, smells, colours, even the taste and feel of all these, all co-existed in a multi-faceted experience.

Suddenly this myriad experience coalesced into a terrible

scream. I saw it, a vivid, blue-scarlet flash of lightning jagging instantly across my mind. I woke up to see one of the clergy forcing his finger at the Boy who stood, his face like a girl's, shadowless, looking up into a strong beam of sunlight coming from a window high in the cloister-wall. The clergyman's face worked ferociously as he screamed a second time. Others in the group began to be distressed. They stared at the Boy who turned to scrutinise their faces. He was alarmed and startled. As he turned, his face weirdly became a boy's. Several backed away from him. He became troubled. He searched for my face. I went towards him. Another clergyman screamed. Someone else began to laugh, a dry, frightening laugh.

The supervisor hurried from one to the other, trying to reassure them. He coupled the calm ones with the distressed, turning to me to ask with his eyes to help. I went to the Boy who was weeping, but still looking from face to face. One of the older women came up to him, towering over him in a comic-threatening gesture. Her idiotic stance made me very angry. I wanted to hit her, bang her to the ground.

The Boy took my hand. I led him away from the group into the cathedral. We sat for a minute near the altar. I asked him if he was alright. He assented, his eyes and face very troubled.

It took nearly an hour to reassure the group and redirect their scattered attention back onto sweet experiences. I think the gargoyles which turned me on kind of turned their trip sour, even after they had got over the Boy. I suggested this to the supervisor, who glanced up at the gargoyles, assenting half-heartedly. He explained that they had used the cloisters for nearly two years and only occasionally had one or two of the group reacted to them.

"The Boy started it, I know," I said.

"You say he hasn't been given a name?"

I nodded. "He's been brought up very freely."

"Don't worry," he said, "I don't think it's his fault really . . . er . . . do you think he's at all maladjusted?"

"Do you think," I said hotly, indicating the group, "that any of them is?"

He looked into my face. "All of them must be," I went on, "to rely on chemical happiness."

"Come and join us sometimes, and find out for yourself," he suggested.

We walked home. I was tempted to ask the Boy what he thought about the group, but something in his manner suggested that I shouldn't. When we got home he seemed ill-at-ease.

"You can video-phone Mary, you know," I said.

"I think I'd like to draw."

When David and Jill arrived that evening, carrying lots of food, the Boy was absorbed in drawing the interior of the caves at Les Eysies. I was writing. Both David and Jill, still holding their parcels, came in to see him.

The Boy got up and went to each in turn, looking into their faces and shaking their hands. David laughed nervously.

Jill asked, "Is your mother with you?"

David said, at the same time, "I 'ope you're hungry. What's your name?"

"I haven't got a name."

"Well, in that case I'll call you nipper." David paused, looked at me, and asked if the Boy was having him on. I shook my head.

"I don't mind being called nipper by one person for a day or so."

Jill asked, "Would you like to have a permanent name?"

"I think I'll choose one soon," the Boy said sadly.

"Is your mother . . . is Mary Johnson with you?" Jill asked again.

"No, Jill," the Boy said, "but I can video-phone if I wish."

"I'm going to cook some food," Jill said, "are you hungry?"

He nodded his head gravely. "Can I help you?" he asked. Jill took his hand and led him out to the kitchen.

"How's my wife?" I asked David.

"She's great . . . and you don't have to worry about me there," he said.

"You mean . . ."

"Listen, you're my mate . . . you don't think I'd foul me own nest, do you? And I'd go about it subtle, like, wouldn't I?"

"You mean . . ."

"Anyway she'd never take me. She's a bit snobbish, your ex-missus. But I like being with her. And I think she likes being with me."

I wandered out of the room.

Just as we sat down to eat supper, the video-phone buzzed. It was Margaret, wanting to know if John and Annie could come down.

I assented.

"Annie wants to bring a few of her friends."

"That's OK."

"I like that Boy."

"He said you were against love."

"He said I'm in sin."

"Well, don't sound so pleased about it."

"But that's why I get these heads . . . and why I'm so irritable. My life's all wrong."

"Bloody hell," I said—humorously, I hope—"I've been telling you for years your life's all wrong."

"Yes, but he's so clever . . . helpful. He didn't tell me, he let me find out for myself. You used to try to stick it down my throat. I knew my life was all wrong . . . that's why I left you."

"How's Annie today?"

"Oh, she and I had a good weep. I went into her bedroom this morning. She obviously hadn't slept well. We cuddled. I told her how bad I felt last night. She's alright. We're all alright, I suppose. It's you."

"What's me?"

"We're alright. It's just you who's got serious problems."

"Did the Boy tell you that?"

"He let me work it out for myself. I've promised myself that I'll do my best to help you."

"Great. When are the kids coming?"
"They're on their way. 'Bye."

I went back into the breakfast room.

Jill was dreaming, David was destroying food, his jaws moving fiercely, rapidly, the next huge mouthful poised on his fork, ready to be plunged into his mouth.

The Boy was sitting self-contained, listening to his inner voices. Very quietly, I said to him: "My wife tells me you think I've got serious problems."

He turned to look at me, slowly bringing himself back. Jill said, "I feel stoned . . . it's beautiful."

She hadn't eaten her food. I felt the force of the Boy's personality as he searched my face, at the same time thinking extensively of what he was going to say. David, mouth bulging, said, inclining his head towards the Boy: "Does he know the food he's eating is nicked?"

Jill turned to look at David:

"It doesn't matter to him where it came from or who thinks he owns it."

I was still absorbed in the awful rapport between the Boy and me. His face changed expression several times, the feelings flitting kind of across his face like the images from a film-strip. I waited, sweating. He stood up. "You have many fears," he said slowly. "Of death . . . of knowledge . . . of anger . . ."

"Jesus!" David exclaimed.

"Yes?" the Boy answered.

Jill cracked out laughing. I began to laugh slowly. The Boy's face relaxed into a smile. When he began to laugh, my control cracked and I bellowed with laughter, tears covering my face. David also.

"Thank God," I spluttered, feeling for a handkerchief, "you've got a sense of humour. That's the first funny thing I've heard you say." I looked at him. I can't describe his face. Full of concern, love, knowledge, sadness. I felt the stretching tearing of the guts.

"Well, Jesus, what do fink of my cooking?" David asked, heavily cheerful.

"The food tasted better in France."

"But you've eaten it all."

"I was hungry."

"I stole it . . . the food you've eaten."

"Is that what 'nicked' means?"

"Yeah . . . nicked, stolen. Most of what we eat here is nicked."

"You think that's important," the Boy observed quietly.

"If I thought it was important I wouldn't do it," David said. He looked at me, making a gesture towards the Boy: "He talks like a grown-up."

"He's only lived with grown-ups," I explained.

"I think I see what you mean," David said to the Boy.

Annie, her friends, and John came into the hall. The Boy heard them and got up immediately.

"Thank you," he said to David, "for stealing and cooking my food."

He went out to the kids. I heard Annie introducing him, helped by John. Annie named each of them, then she explained to them that he hadn't a name.

"We've got to call you something," John said.

"No we haven't," Annie replied.

"Call me Jesus," he answered quietly.

There was an uncomfortable silence.

"Would you like to see my drawings?" he asked.

They trooped into the sitting room.

"That's not fair," said Jill. "We forced it on him."

"I'm inclined to let him take care of himself," I said.

"He thanked me for stealing . . . did you hear?"

"He's beautiful," Jill said quietly.

"Does he really think he's Jesus?"

"It's more who we think he is . . . and how much he can join us in our thoughts," I said. I felt stretched, disturbed. Guilty, even.

"He's so free," Jill said, "that we'll force him to be further and further away from us."

"And calling him Jesus is the first step?" I asked her.

"It was me," David said proudly.

In the sitting room I found all the kids drawing. The Boy's drawings were lying around on the floor. He was talking with John.

"Everything OK?" I asked the Boy.

"Smashing," he said.

John's face registered tremendous pleasure: "That's my word," he said proudly.

The kids didn't want to leave when a father arrived in a car to take them home. His daughter urged him into the sitting room to meet the Boy. I followed them in.

"This is my dad," she said.

The Boy held out his hands. She went on:

"This is a friend of Annie's daddy. He's called Jesus."

The father avoided the Boy's hands with a clumsy, sharp movement, seized his daughter's and led her out. He told two other girls that he'd been asked to give them a lift. They got up and followed without saying anything. I wanted to intervene but I saw from the Boy's face that it was unnecessary. The front door slammed. Annie said, "That's awful . . . I'm sorry."

"He nicked his daughter," the Boy said, smiling.

Annie went towards him: "But it's not right . . ."

In the kitchen I asked Jill—she was washing up—if I could sleep with her.

She shook her head.

"You ought to," I went on lightly. "What will they all think of me when they find out he sleeps in my bed?"

"Why shouldn't he?"

"That's not my point . . . what will people think? I'll be lynched."

She laughed lightly: "A lot of people ostracise me because I live here . . . it's rather good."

I smiled but I was perturbed.

He was asleep when I got into bed. His body nestled up to mine as I settled between the sheets.

I felt most awkward.

The first school I took the Boy to was mine. Kitchen—the man who had been appointed in my place—met us by arrangement. He was put out by the visit.

He owed much to me. I had both appointed him to the school as a head-of-department in the first place, and supported his application for my job in the second. And yet already at this stage he showed strong hostility towards me. Part of this was, I learned later, because Jill had been a favourite pupil of his for years. But he also had very strong, not-to-say hysterical feelings about the Boy. In their beautifully-conducted and terribly-successful campaign to whip up national interest in the trial of Alistair and me, Alistair's 'Oxford' twins, Emma and Sybil, interviewed Kitchen. This interview, with his pious yet vicious opinions, was networked in Europe, I understand.

(I still don't understand all that I'm about to describe. I don't know just at what stage Emma and Sybil decided to make Alistair and me, together with Mary and the Boy, the centre of their huge campaign which even now seems to me to have been aimed at the Government rather than at a spiritual rebirth. From the moment I woke up in hospital to the day of the Assizes, I felt taken on by events with no more understanding than a bewildered bull in a crowded bull-ring. All I can do is describe austerely, without interpretation, the incidents that led to the 'massacre of the innocents' as Mary called it. My part in the killings, my responsibility, others must judge.)

The Boy, I noticed as we approached Kitchen in the entrance-hall, was again walking with the movements of a girl.

"Peculiar . . . no name. I'd heard he called himself Jesus," Kitchen said sharply as he led us towards the Biology Block. He spoke as if the Boy wasn't there.

"You think all this is crazy," I observed.

"I've too much respect for you to think that," he articulated unctuously. "After all, who better than me to know your judgement is good. But I do admit there are ugly rumours about already."

"Wait till he's grown up", I said, unaware of the incidents that were almost on us. Kitchen looked at me, hesitating to speak his mind, then hurried on.

The first thing that caught the Boy's attention in the Biology laboratory was a microscope. Kitchen left us as the Biology teacher showed the Boy various slides that had been prepared. The Boy peered at them one by one, adjusting the microscope each time he replaced a slide. I went over to him.

"There are so few teachers," he said, fiddling with the microscope. "And the children all seem to be doing the same thing."

"But one must have systematic teaching," the teacher said.

"Who chooses the system?"

"Well, I do. I've pretty well as much freedom as I like . . . subject to the syllabus."

"Do they mind?"

"Who . . . the kids? I don't ask them. If I asked them we'd end up nowhere . . . each kid would want his own syllabus and then where would we be!"

"Do they remember what you teach them?"

"Well, to be perfectly honest, I don't think they do. But they've had a chance to develop an interest. And of course, some of them will become teachers themselves."

"They'll remember that you didn't ask them what they wanted to do, and made them do what you thought."

I butted in, "But they'll get something surely. They won't forget everything. And even if they do, there's a lot of security in this situation. And things are changing so much outside that a few years of security aren't wasted."

"Yes, but it's security that they get by not thinking their own thoughts and by doing what teachers want. By wanting to do what teachers want. They diminish a bit in school."

The teacher asked, "You think I should ask every pupil what he wants to do?"

"Yes, and keep asking them because they'll change their minds a lot, I suppose."

"Oh, so kids are more important than teachers!"

"I'm a kid, but I don't think that my feelings are more important than yours. But if I want to learn something, and you wish to teach me, then you have to ask me what it is."

"That's just it. Most of them don't want to learn. If I wasn't here what do you think would go on in this lab.? Pandemonium. As you say, you are a child and with all respect to Mr Foster, I don't think you should come here thinking you know it all."

"You're trying to make me ashamed," the Boy said quietly.

"Nonsense. But I've been doing this work for seventeen years."

"You think what I say is nonsense," the Boy replied.

"But you've no experience. That preparation you were looking at, that took time and thought to prepare."

"I was interested in the microscope. It creates knowledge."

"Now that's what I call real nonsense. It's just an instrument."

I said, "It's not such nonsense, surely?"

"I think it is," the teacher said, "and this is my subject. We've got a little anarchist on our hands," the teacher added.

"Are all teachers like that?" the Boy asked as we entered the school dining hall. "They can't be," he went on. I noticed that he was keen not to sit at the staff-table and drifted easily towards tables where kids about his own age were sitting.

Towards the end of the meal, I glanced over to him. He was sitting on the table surrounded by boys and girls of all ages. They kept asking questions and he answered slowly, solemnly.

Two supervisors hovered anxiously near him. They both knew me, and respected him as my guest but felt agitated by this 'abuse' of the dining hall. They had to get the tables cleared by a certain time.

The members of staff sitting with me had been mute as always, during meals. Several now found the situation amusing. One or two were distressed by the Boy's presence but out of either loyalty to me, or scruple of some kind, forbore from reacting.

One of the older pupils explained to the Boy that the supervisors were upset and he was led out onto the playing field. They sat him on the cricket-roller, an object the need for which was explained to him by several enthusiasts. Then the questioning began again.

While replying, from where I stood, he seemed grave, simple, and produced quietness among the mass of pupils. More pupils streamed across to join the crowd round him.

When the bell went for the afternoon session, he came over to me while the rest went into school.

My ex-secretary reported that the headmaster had been called away suddenly to the Education Office and would I mind showing the Boy anything more he wanted to see.

The Boy was delighted with the language laboratories, disgusted by the counselling department, totally intrigued by the tiny space-laboratory, and was delighted again with the gymnasium.

He stripped off naked and went to join the class that was working. His nakedness caused a lot of pointing and giggling—the class were girls—but the teacher, glancing at me helplessly, didn't feel that anything too terrible was happening.

The Boy joined in, dancing with the girls, his face serious, his mind absorbed by the complicated movements his body was learning. He moved beautifully. Watching him, I became sexually excited.

"He's a natural," the PE teacher said to me. "Is he queer?"

"He's both a boy and a girl."

"His genitals are really attractive," she said, impulsively. Like many PE teachers, she used words awkwardly. "All his body. He moves beautifully. He's absolutely a natural. I wish I could have him for a year or two."

"Did you see him after lunch?" She shook her head. "Talking to nearly the whole school."

"Your successor must have been pleased!" she said. "Can he swim?"

"You'd better ask him."

The girls were showing him a Greek dance. One or two, behind his back, still whispered about his nakedness, but he was so alert with his body, and danced with them so easily, that after a short time they were absorbed completely in the dance. And so were the teacher and I, watching.

When Kitchen bustled in, looking for us, we were startled, as if wakened out of a dream. He stopped short, his face hardening hysterically, when he saw the Boy's nakedness. He stamped towards us. The dancing stopped. No-one spoke for some time. Then one or two of the girls nervously encouraged each other to slip out of the gym. Kitchen stared at the Boy who looked at the faces of the girls, then at mine.

"You'd better put your clothes on," I said.

"Foster," Kitchen said hoarsely. "Can I have a word with you? Do you mind?" He led me out of the gym. He was very upset. "That's as much as I can stand. I insist that you accept responsibility for any repercussions. I must say you've gone too far. Far far too far. I want you off the premises."

"Aw fuck off," I said, trying to keep control.

He went on: "It's widely known there's something seriously wrong with you, Foster."

I stopped and turned to face him. He swallowed a couple of times, then said, "Apart from being a chronic bore, which you've always been, there's something psychotic about your brazen and total disregard for the standards you used to work for. I taught Jill. She was a terribly attractive girl. And she had a good mind."

"What's Jill got to do with it?"

"I've had my instructions. From the office."

"Instructions from the Education Officer . . . that idiot!"

"I happen to value his advice. And he was giving me more than his personal opinion. There's so much hate against you in this school, I'm surprised you came back."

This worried me. He smelt that he'd got through. He went on: "I've heard how you talk about your wife . . . your ex-wife. But I'd have thought you would think at least twice before damaging your children. Their lives are here in this town. They can't leave, no matter how unhappy their father makes them."

I went towards him, strangely emotional, my throat full. He continued, "There's more to breaking conventional morality, dull though it may be for some, than shooting your mouth off at impressionable young girls. I doubt if you'll ever get a job again."

"You're mixing up spitefulness and jealousy with a good point or two," I spoke slowly, the words forcing themselves out of my mouth. I reached out and took hold of his arms. Shook him violently. He went complacently limp. I shook him again. A group of pupils were watching.

"Listen," I said, "if you tell me what you mean about my work being undermined by what I've done, I'll listen to you."

I was speaking through my teeth. My voice thick in my throat.

Despite having lost weight I was still a big fellow. He began to realise I might harm him. His face turned white. I went on: "If you can tell me how my children are damaged by my behaviour, then I'll listen, you stupid, unspeakable . . . you might . . ." I shook him again, my face within an inch of his. ". . . help me to relieve things. But if you think you can frighten me by these obscene, disgusting insinuations . . ."

"Then he's quite right," said the Boy quietly.

I let go of Kitchen. He staggered, rubbed his arms, and stepped away hurriedly. I turned to the Boy. He searched my face. I groaned. I don't quite remember what happened next, but I know I was put in the back of someone's car and driven home.

I remember clearly going into my bedroom and shutting the door.

That evening a lot of kids arrived at the house. I heard much activity but was left alone. I kept waking up from troubled sleep, expecting to find the Boy beside me. It was three or four in the morning before he got into bed. He kissed me goodnight and went immediately to sleep.

I woke up, dazed and tired, the next morning and lay there, dreaming, talking to myself, sorting things out, then re-sorting them, going over and over again, justifications to my children, to Jill's parents, to Jill's friends, to my ex-pupils, even to Kitchen.

I got up about twelve and went to make coffee. There was a note from David saying that a police inspector had been to see me and he'd told him to clear off until he got a warrant. He'd added that if they came back I was to ring him and tell them nothing.

I immediately video-phoned the police and eventually got the Inspector who wanted to see me. He told me that Kitchen had made a complaint against me and while there might be nothing to it, it would help if I made a statement. The Inspector agreed to come straight away.

They weren't armed. At first, the Inspector was apologetic. The police constable with him put me on oath and took down my description of what had happened. I admitted getting hold of Kitchen, shaking him, using abusive language and generally being passionately silly. The Inspector was more or less for me until it became clearer that there had been children present. I, perhaps foolishly, mentioned the Boy as one of the witnesses. The Inspector wanted to know the name of the Boy. From that moment, he was cold and reserved. Even more foolishly, I tried to explain that the Boy had no name and in a sense no parents either. Both policemen exchanged rapid glances.

"He sleeps here?" the Inspector said, implicitly imputing criminal activities.

"What do you want to know?" I asked.

"Can we see his bed?"

"Why do you want to see his bed?"

"I'd like to see where he sleeps."

"With me," I admitted weakly.

"And how old is he, sir?" the Inspector asked.

"Eleven. I think you'd better . . ."

"If you don't mind, sir, I don't want advice from you. Does he wear pyjamas?"

"Do you have the right to ask questions like these?"

"I've the right to ask you any questions. You have the right to refuse to answer. But of course, if you refuse, then a certain interpretation may be put upon your refusal."

"Well, there's absolutely nothing to hide. What do you want to know?"

"Does he wear pyjamas of any sort?"

"He sleeps naked. We both sleep naked."

"In a double bed?"

I nodded. "Do you want to know if I fuck him?"

There was a long pause. I said impatiently, "Come on Inspector, you've heard the word before. You use it yourself often. That's the crunch, isn't it?"

"Well, that's not quite how I would have put the question but . . ."

"Of course not. You must meet the Boy. He's beautiful . . . I mean, he's a true person. No-one in their right minds would abuse him."

The Inspector asked me to repeat what I'd said so the other could get it down. Then he asked, "Is there any physical contact between you and the Boy?"

I hesitated.

"Do you kiss him?"

"I have kissed him. Have you got kids of your own?"

"But this Boy isn't a child of yours," he said.

"Look, Inspector, don't be difficult. You kiss your kids. If you were French you'd kiss everybody everytime you met them. I kiss him as I kiss my sons and daughter."

"And he kisses you in the same way?"

"Of course."

"You say he has no parents."

"Not in the way that your kids and my kids have."

"I live with my children," he said.

"Good for them . . . and for you. The Boy lives with his mother, only she isn't really a mother. Also there are two men, her father and her . . . husband. Wait till you meet the Boy, you'll see immediately that all this questioning is totally irrelevant."

I again had to repeat what I'd said slowly and it was written down. I signed it. He left, promising to come the next morning to see the Boy.

"You're a total bloody idiot," Alistair said over the video-phone.

"But I'm not afraid of the truth."

"What's the truth? They'll do you all ends up. Let's keep cool about this. Have you told Mary?"

"Should I bother?"

"Of course. Immediately."

"I thought I'd wait until they'd met the Boy. It could all fizzle."

"Once they get a whiff of buggery, darling, they involve the Chief Constable, the Social Welfare department, the civil servant in charge of buggery at the Ministry . . . the lot. Corrupting a minor gets them all hot under the collar. Have you a solicitor?"

"Yes, but he'd be hopeless."

"He couldn't have done worse than you."

"You think I should speak to Mary?"

"Immediately. And Anthony Johnson might know somebody who could help."

"You think it's serious."

"Let me put it this way. Go out this minute and buy him some pyjamas, a bed if there isn't a spare one and get him into a room of his own."

"He's not that kind of boy."

"What do you mean?"

"He is a true person . . . you know, he won't want to evade . . . hide his behaviour."

"But he's a complete child! He's been protected all his few years . . . he won't refuse to sleep in another room, surely."

"Why don't you come over and meet him?"

"Excellent. I'll come straight away."

"I'll wait here for you."

"No," he said, "go out and get that bed."

I 'phoned Mary immediately. She listened carefully, looking straight into the camera. She asked, "How long will it take me to get to your house?"

"If you go to Amiens there's an hourly Monorail through the Tunnel to Leeds. I can't meet you, I'm afraid, I haven't a car."

"Jane might meet me. If not I'll take a taxi. I think I'll go to Jane's anyway. I'll ring you from there as soon as possible."

"Do you think he should go on sleeping in my bed?"

"Of course if he wants to. Don't worry. It's silly saying don't worry, but don't about the Boy. He's all right. Don't involve solicitors at this stage. Oh, have you told Christopher?"

"I thought that might make things worse. I don't even know if you and he are married."

"Tell him straight away. Oh, don't. I'll ring Jane now. One more thing, Tony, why don't you go and see that headmaster and have a talk with him?"

"Good idea. It's good talking to you."

She smiled, leaned to kiss me through the camera, and we switched off.

"Where've you been?" I asked the Boy when he got back in the late afternoon.

"I went for lunch to Annie's school. She came here early this morning and invited me."

"How did it go?"

"I like English children. They're super."

"I'm in a bit of trouble."

I explained fully, telling him the Inspector wanted to ask about where he slept.

"It bothers everybody . . . where people sleep," he said.

"Mary's coming over."

"Oh, good. I'd rather like to have my supper at David's café. Will you come?"

"I'm expecting a friend."

"Grown up?"

"I'm afraid so."

Alistair was awkward when he came that evening. He tried not to stare at the Boy. He was immediately so impressed that I thought he might kneel down at his feet.

Alistair jerked his head round to look at me. "I haven't brought my frankincense," he said. The Boy approached him. Alistair added: "You live near Beauvais. I may come and live near you. I know your grandmother, Jane Johnson. She's a close friend of mine. I've known about you since you were born. Before. I'm glad to meet you. Have you eaten?"

We decided to go to David's café for a fry-up.

"What's a fry-up?" the Boy asked.

"Why don't you wait and see," Alistair said kindly.

David was very pleased when we arrived. He put two tables together, told Jill, who was working, to take off her overall and sit down. He provided us with a marvellous fry-up. He kept looking at me and laughing.

Towards the end of the supper he called across: "Did you do what I told you?"

"What was that?"

"Give them a blank sheet." I shook my head.

He looked immediately very angry, concerned, then pitying.

"You daft cunt," he said, then, after glancing at the Boy, he added, "and that's swearing."

"My words exactly," said Alistair, drily.

"Does it matter?" asked Jill. "After all, nothing's wrong . . . no crime's been committed."

"That," I said, satisfied for the opportunity, "is what Mary Johnson said."

David, still calling, "Do what I did . . . plead guilty to common assault. All they can do is bind you over to keep the peace, and if you want that soft cunt of a headmaster handled properly like, I'll get one or two of my mates to rough him up a bit."

"Thanks," I said, sardonically.

Alistair asked, gesturing to David: "Who's this desperate character?"

David smiled and called out from near the bar: "I'm a life-long, petty crook. Reformed. Straight as a die."

The Boy was looking at David very affectionately.

David glanced at him and asked:

"Isn't that right, Jesus? You know I don't nick nowt."

"I like your voice, David, but I don't understand much of what you say."

"Hear that?" said David proudly to the whole café, "Jesus here likes my voice."

The next morning the Inspector and his colleague were reluctant to carry out their interview with Alistair present but I insisted and called the Boy into the room. Both policemen stared hard at him. Instantly I felt hostility in them towards the Boy. So did Alistair. We both became very aggressive. I think the police sensed this straight away. There we were then, all kind of bristling and trying not to bristle, with the Boy in the middle looking round from face to face. I explained to the Boy that these gentlemen wished to ask him questions. The Inspector spoke first:

"Mr Foster tells me you don't have a Christian name."

"I'm thinking of having one."

"But how do you know who you are?"

"I sort of change a lot."

"Look here, young man, are you trying to be difficult?"

I burst in, stepping towards the Inspector aggressively, "No, he's not!"

The Inspector measured me up with his eyes, planning some kind of destructive comment. The Boy said, speaking very quietly, "I am difficult to understand because I feel and think so many different things." The Inspector continued to stare destructively into my face.

At that stage I really felt he stood for everything I hated. I wanted to jolt all his stiff stupidities out of him. As we stared at each other, I saw his face as a boy, then the kind of mother he had, and the father. I saw echelons of alienating experiences folding implacably over him as a young person, looping so tightly around him that life became a mental strait-jacket within which only very restricted thoughts and feelings were possible, and any attempt to move beyond these not only was unalterably contained, but also stimulated terrible tensions.

The Boy came over and took my hand in both his. The Inspector glanced down at our hands, thought for a while, his eyes lowered, then asked: "How do people talk to you who want to ask you things?"

"It's not difficult after a bit."

"Have you any parents?"

"Not in the way that English or French children have."

The Inspector glanced questioningly at the constable. "I wish I knew what to call him," he said. The Constable nodded. I know what to call you, I thought.

"Some people have started to call me Jesus," the Boy explained.

This upset both policemen. Alistair stepped to my side. The Constable and Inspector were in line now. I felt the Boy through my hand. He was alarmed, frightened. I looked down into his face. He was staring at the police. I half-realised that he knew exactly how we all felt. By now I was bursting to violate, to mutilate the Inspector if he offered the slightest grounds for doing so. I remember my legs shaking violently. I knew instinctively that Alistair, hunched powerfully beside me, was an instant ally.

"Where do you normally live?" the Inspector asked.

"With Mary, Anthony and Christopher in a little village in France."

"And who's Mary?"

" 'is muther," the Constable cracked, sneeringly.

"That's right!" I articulated, fiercely.

"Look, sir," the Inspector said to me, "do you mind?"

The Boy said, "You would call her my mother but she's not really. She's a lot of people but she looks after me in some things."

"I see. You live with Mary who's your mother but isn't because she's a lot of people. Well, I think I've got that down. What about the others . . . what are they called?"

"Well, Anthony is Mary's father and Christopher sleeps with Mary and me but I don't think you would call him my father though . . ."

The Inspector flinched, anger jerking his body and making his movements bizarre. I could hardly stop lashing out at him. The Boy looked into his face: "You don't like to know how we live. You ask but it makes you angry." The Inspector couldn't speak. He stared down at the Boy, his eyes bulging. He turned impulsively to the Constable and made a cruel, cynical gesture of contempt for the Boy. Alistair and I shifted forward dangerously. The Inspector seemed too big for his uniform. He suddenly screamed at the Boy, raising his open hand to smack him viciously. Alistair grunted, grateful for the opportunity. He banged the Inspector a tremendous blow on the head. As the Constable tried to interfere, I seized him, belabouring his head.

The four of us fought desperately, each trying to inflict the most damage. I can't remember the sequence of events. At some stage the two policemen gained the upper hand. Alistair and I were held down separately on the floor. The Constable was hitting me with his truncheon. I was able to shield my head. He began to hit at my genitals, mouthing venomously:

"Cunt . . . fucking, shitting prick . . . I'll put this into you . . ."

The Inspector was hitting deliberately at Alistair's face, trying to smash his fist into Alistair's nose and eyes.

I gather it was before this stage that Mary came into the room.

The mad display continued. I could shield myself reasonably well from being hurt. I think Alistair could also. We both rolled about under our attackers. I was quite light-headed. I smiled at one stage, saying to Alistair: "We've beaten them at their own game."

As Alistair started to answer, the policeman on me leaned across and hit him a terrible blow on the back of the head. Alistair's head jerked forward as if his neck had collapsed.

I reached up signalling it was time to stop. It was at this stage that I glimpsed Mary. I was very surprised to see her. It was unreal that she should be in my home. I started to get up onto my feet.

The next thing I knew was that I had a massive headache. I opened my eyes, moving my head slowly. Immediately the room spun fiercely from side to side. I stiffened, seizing hold of the bed, steadying myself, eyes closed. I heard someone say that I was coming round. I kept my eyes closed until the spinning stopped. I opened them slowly. I was in a hospital ward.

The nurses were very helpful. They explained that I had had a nasty blow on the head and I was to stay still. I described my symptoms but they weren't at all worried. It was clear that they didn't think I was very badly hurt.

Dr Seymore-Cartwright came in later in the day. I was pretty quick to tell him about the dizziness. He explained that there was a bit of internal bleeding and the dizziness—vertigo he called it—would go on for some time.

"What happened?" I asked.

"What do you remember?"

"Seeing Mary Johnson, unreal, in my house."

"Nothing else?" he asked.

I shook my head. It was a mistake. I had to cling to the bed, my eyes tightly closed, until the dizziness slowed down.

"What happened?" I asked again.

"You got an almighty crack on the head. For saying something rather rude to Mary Johnson about the police, I think. There was another little melée only Alistair couldn't help you. He has a broken neck . . . at least, one of the vertebrae is cracked."

"What about Mary and the Boy?"

"Oh, they're alright. They're both living at your house at the moment. It's full each evening with youngsters."

"How long have I been here?"

"Two nights but I kept you asleep. I've arranged for some tests today but really I think that there's not much seriously wrong with you." He removed the covers from my bed and gave me a thorough physical examination, reassuring me repeatedly that everything was working.

"They'll X-ray you and do a few more things, none of them horrible, but you're alright."

"I'd like to see my kids."

He nodded. I went on: "What a mess."

"I'll telephone your wife and ask her to send your children."

"I feel bloody sorry for myself."

"Well, don't worry about your head. I can get that right for you."

We shook hands.

"Could you ask Margaret to send the kids today?"

I had a day of electrical and neurological examinations of my head. Early in the evening Seymore-Cartwright called in again to say that he'd spoken to Margaret. "Oh," he went on, "the Police want to interview you. I told them you'd probably be coherent tomorrow . . . what do you think?"

"Are they going ahead with that fuss over Kitchen?"

He nodded, watching my face.

"There's something else?" I asked.

He nodded again, unsure of what to say.

"Tell me all," I said smiling.

"I think they intend to prefer serious charges against you, I don't know quite which. You seem to have broken so many laws at once."

"Against me?"

"And Alistair Shuttleworth."

"Is he here?"

Seymore-Cartwright assented.

"Can I see him?"

"Of course."

He called for the nurse who attached a video-phone to the television set and dialled the number that Seymore-Cartwright gave her. The camera at Alistair's end was a bit out of focus at first and he seemed very ill, propped up in his bed with a plastic collar supporting his neck. I couldn't face the camera in my room, so he was speaking to the back of my head. He pointed at me, laughing. As his camera came into focus it was clear he was in good form.

"What a fucking comedy," were his first words. "Are you on your own?"

I shook my head and went into a spin, groping desperately to hold onto the bed.

"You all right?" he asked, concerned.

"Yes . . . I just get dizzy spells. How about you?"

"*They* broke my bloody neck. And now they've charged *me* with grievous bodily harm!"

"Isn't that serious?"

"Well, that depends on lots of things. They're taking it seriously. You're going to be charged as well. We both apparently interfered with the police in the doing of their duty . . ."

"I feel terrible," I said.

"I've decided to do without a solicitor," he said.

"They could send us to prison."

"Have you seen Mary or the Boy?"

"Not yet. I haven't seen my own kids yet."

"I'm seeing her tomorrow. Do you want to see her?"

"As soon as possible," I said.

Annie came on her own the following day.

"I can't stay long because mummy doesn't like my being here," she said.

"I understand."

She kissed me gently. I gathered her into my arms. We hugged silently for some time.

"I still go down to the old house . . . to your house," she said.

"You like the Boy," I observed.

"Lots of us do. The house is full . . . every evening. Lots more would come if their parents would let them."

"What do you all do?"

"Nothing, really. We talk. Mary and . . ."

Annie hesitated.

". . . and that Boy and Jill, your girl-friend. . . ."

Annie looked at me.

"Jill's a very nice girl," I said.

"I know that . . . her and David. David's terribly nice. He comes to see Mummy a lot. Every day. He brings us eggs."

"They've been stolen. I think Mummy ought not to take them."

"He pays for them. He said so. He's not a crook any more."

"He's a nice guy," I admitted.

"He tells us stories."

"David?"

"No, at your . . . the Boy Jesus."

"What about?"

"About a boy and a girl who haven't any parents . . . not real parents. It's a bit like 'Dr Who'. . . that and 'Treasure Island' all mixed up."

A nurse came in and indicated that it was time for Annie to go. I said: "Don't upset mummy but come again as soon as possible."

"I'd like to," Annie said.

Later Mary and the Boy came. Mary asked me about my head while the Boy looked round the room in the same way he'd looked round the caves at Les Eysies. They settled down in chairs.

I didn't know what to say.

We were silent for some time, possibly ten or twelve minutes. I think I even dozed a little. There was no sense of strain, of having to think of things to say. I asked, "You're staying at home?"

"We thought it was good to be here until Alistair and you have recovered," Mary said.

"I wish it was all over," I said hurriedly.

"This is just the start," Mary said.

The Boy came and sat on the bed. I felt for his hand and held onto it tightly.

"I'm not conscious of what's going on but I know that it's important," I said.

"You'll make an excellent witness," Mary observed drily.

I smiled. So did she.

"So Alistair's told you we're being charged."

She nodded.

"What happened?" I asked.

"It's very hard to know," she answered. "In simple terms you tried to kill the police inspector. I think he invited your violence. You're both violent men. I think each of you was profoundly threatened by the other."

"Are you sure I tried to kill him?"

"That was one of your intentions." She smiled. "There may have been others. I've spoken to Mr Kitchen. He thinks you were very disturbed when you were at his school."

"Did I hurt the inspector?"

"His jaw was broken."

I glanced at my right hand.

"Then the other policeman gave you a solid whack on your head."

I think I apologised but I'm not sure. Something I said made Mary observe, coldly I thought at the time, "I've always known terrible things would happen around us."

"You've been to see Margaret," I said, thinking, no doubt of 'terrible things'.

Mary nodded.

"What did she say?" I asked.

"She was determined I should see what she calls 'her side'."

"That's easy to understand."

"Your children, they . . ."

I watched her while she thought carefully what to say: ". . . they love her but they don't believe everything she would like them to believe."

"Michael . . . the eldest?"

"He told me he hates you. It's good that he can say things like that."

"He sometimes says that he wishes I would die . . . I don't know whether I can put up with his feelings."

"Is that all he feels?" Mary asked.

I thought for a minute, then said: "You mean he feels other things as well . . . I see what you mean."

The Boy smiled and said: "David is super."

We all smiled. I asked Mary: "What do you think I ought to do?"

"Alistair thinks he can make a *cause célèbre* out of this."

"What do you think?"

"I don't feel involved."

"You mean you want nothing to do with us?"

"Oh, I want to help. I may not be of much help but whatever I can do I will."

She looked at the Boy and continued: "But I don't wish to become involved in Alistair's plans. He intends to organise public opinion. I don't feel the need to be other than the person I am . . . I mean, to do things other than those which interest me."

"You started all this but you don't want to . . ." I stopped.

"Alistair wants to put the whole of society on trial . . . to publicise the issues—what he takes to be the issues. He's a media-man. I wish to be associated only with what I do."

"You'll be a witness?"

"Sure."

"That'll be a public act."

She assented. I went on: "But you mean it will make no difference to you whether Alistair publicises . . . organises publicity or not."

"It makes no difference to me," she said.

"That's terrible," I heard myself say. I turned to the Boy: "What do you think?"

He searched my face.

"I feel that you don't really know what to do," he said.

I asked Mary: "Do you think that he should be a witness?"

She looked at the Boy, who said, "Of course."

"You understand what it could involve?" I asked.

"No," he answered.

"Neither do I," I said.

Silence. I continued, "It's all so difficult . . . obscure."

I turned from them.

"Do you ever listen to your inner voices?" Mary asked.

"I talk to myself constantly . . . I wish I could stop."

"Do you ever listen?" she insisted.

That was the end of our conversation. We sat, presumably all three listening to our inner voices. I found I was justifying myself over and over again. To Margaret, the kids . . . Kitchen . . . to a court-of-law.

Early next morning, David arrived.

"How's Margaret?" I asked him.

He grinned, his eyes cold, watchful. "I see her every evening . . . well, most evenings. She's great . . .'ates your guts for what she thinks you're doing to her and the kids . . . Michael hates you . . . at least, he says he does. He says he'll visit you in prison."

That silenced me. He went on: "I think that lot . . . you know, Mary, Christopher, Jesus . . . I know he isn't Jesus, it's just a joke innit . . . but I know they're all something very special. You know, my life is changing before my very eyes . . . in front of my very eyes. We all kip in your 'ouse, you know."

"Jill?"

He nodded, his eyes narrowing.

"Who does the cooking?"

"Whoever's hungry. I bring a bit back from the café, like. You know, I don't exactly knock it off. It's part of the wages. The gaffer knows I take it."

He was speaking seriously. We both smiled but his eyes were still expressionless.

"Christopher, Mary and me have great talks. And the Boy. Your Annie comes a lot bringing John with her. Margaret doesn't like it but I put your side to her . . ."

"Thanks," I said, ironically.

He paused, then: "I'm right happy. The house is always crammed full of kids. Some nice birds . . ."

"I'm glad you're happy," I said, developing the irony.

"Listen, don't be sarcastic with me. You're gonna be inside and I'm gonna be outside. You'd better show some respect . . ."

He was joking but it made me very angry indeed. I jerked up. My head exploded into violent spinning. I had to ease back, lowering my head slowly, keeping my eyes closed.

David cracked out laughing.

I felt angry, helpless, frightened, stupid.

David stopped laughing, wiping the tears from his eyes.

"What are you gonna do?" he asked. "If I were you I'd . . ."

"I don't know and I don't want any advice."

"I know you don't want advice, but if I were you . . ."

"I don't want any advice."

"Alright," he said, palming me down, "I know what you mean."

"And I know what you mean," I said.

He stopped in the middle of his thoughts, smiling broadly: "You're taking me off, aren't you?"

"Come on, David, think it out. I'm sorry for myself."

"An' you don't want advice from the likes of me . . . well I'll tell you, I've changed . . ."

"What I want from you is cheering up."

"I feel sorry for you, I really do, Tony, honest."

His eyes were strange. Staring, unblinking.

"That doesn't help a bit," I said.

"We're all doing our best for you, you know."

"That doesn't help, either."

He thought for a bit, then, after listening at the door, he brought out half a bottle of brandy. He held it up. He saw my eyes light up. He offered it to me, then took it away just as I was going to get hold of it. "Say please."

I begrudged the way he was playing with me.

"Come on, you miserable old bugger, say please."

I waited.

"You won't get it unless you say please."

"Well, if it means anything, please."

He gave it to me. I broke the seal and unscrewed the cap. The drink made me cough. I passed it over and he cleaned the neck on his handkerchief and drank.

"Do you think he is Jesus? I mean, I know it's a daft question, but there's something very special about him."

I thought for a while. He handed me the bottle.

"It depends on what you think . . . who you think Jesus is."

"He likes me, you know. I mean, he never behaves as if I wasn't worth knowing or anything."

"Exactly."

"I know they aren't his parents, but he sleeps with them. Strange, innit."

I didn't answer.

"I used to dream of . . . you know . . . having it off with my mother . . . do you think that he's . . ." I interjected: "I've dreamt of that. I think it's normal." I had emphasised 'dreamt'.

"I used to look at her tits . . . they used to curtsey, you know, when she walked. I used to toss meself off thinking about her tits . . . putting my face between them."

He laughed very forcibly.

"Perhaps," I said, "if we all had our mothers we'd be fuller or something."

"It's against the law, isn't it?"

"Our father which art in heaven wouldn't have thought so."

"What if one of your sons and . . ."

"I don't know anything about how I would feel . . ."

"They're all such nice people." he said, continuing, "I've started putting money in the till for the food I nick." I smiled: "You mustn't let your boss know. He'd think the world was coming to an end."

"I mean it," he said.

"I know what you mean."

He looked at me, his face breaking into a broad smile, his eyes smiling with the rest.

John came to visit me when David left. He looked at me and was surprised.

"Hello John. Give us a kiss."

He came over and dutifully turned his face so I could kiss him. I hugged him until he got bored and pushed me away. I said:

"You thought I'd be wearing clothes with arrows."

He smiled, his face breaking into a laugh.

"Well," he said, bending sideways and looking up at me, "you are a criminal and sort of in prison."

"Yes. I may even have to go into a real prison."

"Will I be able to come to see you?"

"I think so. Would you like to?"

"It would be great seeing inside a real prison."

He walked around the room, looking at everything.

"Miss Whitehead's on your side."

"Your teacher?"

He nodded: "But I'm on mummy's."

"I'm on mummy's as well. When you get older, you'll learn how to be on lots of sides."

"I know. I think I understand what you want . . . but I love . . ."

He smiled at me then looked away, ". . . mummy more than I love you."

"I love you both."

"I know you always say that but you don't want to live with us."

"Do you think it's possible to love someone and not want to live with them?"

"I don't know," he said, his face very serious. "Does your head hurt?"

"Not much, but if I'm not careful I get dizzy."

"Mine does if I turn round a lot," he said.

"What do you think of the Boy?"

"He's great . . . but he doesn't like playing at war. I love it."

He looked at me for disapproval.

"But he likes playing with you," I said.

"He tells great stories . . . they're soppy but I like them . . . Annie says that he's going to be Jesus. Is he?"

"I don't know . . . what do you think?"

"If he does, how will they kill him?"

"That's not a bad question."

"They can't crucify him, can they now? Daddy, is there ever going to be a war?"

"There's fighting all over, isn't there? Don't you see it?"

"Miss Whitehead thinks that unless everybody stops making weapons there'll be a war in England and we'll all be killed."

"If they didn't make guns and . . ."

"Would you fight?"

"I think in my way I'm fighting."

"I've got to go now," he said with finality.

He tolerated my hugs, gave me a quick kiss, and went out of the room.

Michael had brought him and popped in for a bit. I asked him how things were in the States.

"Getting worse. It's starting in Russia now. Four cities are fighting."

"Each other?"

"I mean within themselves. It'll come here soon. It's inevitable."

"What will you do?" I asked.

"Join the winning side."

"How will you know which is which?"

"I'll join the opposite one to you."

I smiled, genuinely happy that he could produce his aggression so easily and openly.

"I'll be on so many sides at the same time, that you won't know which to oppose."

"I'll think of one."

Silence, then he continued, "Nobody knows what you stand for. But some of my friends are against the police."

I said: "I wish even one person knew what I stand for."

"Then he could tell you." I smiled, nodding. "You know," he went on, "in my mind I'm killing you all the time."

"I wish you'd hurry up and get it out of your mind. I'm dying to teach you to drive and choose good wine."

"I can drive. And I don't use alcohol."

We both smiled. I said:

"That's one thing I thank God for . . . all my kids have got a sense of humour."

"We've got to, with someone like you for a father."

"I know you mean that pejoratively, but I take it as a compliment."

"What does pejorative mean?"

"Something like 'used in a bad sense'."

He nodded, leaning over for a perfunctory kiss, and went towards the door.

"See you in prison," he said.

"It was good seeing you and John."

Alistair trundled his wheel chair into my room about two days later. His neck was still supported by a plastic collar, but he was able to move his head more than I dared move mine.

"Is your neck really broken?" I asked.

"Is anything really anything?" he parried. "Have the police been?"

"They read out the summonses and took away my passport."

"Be bloody nice to them," he said, "because you may need them to protect you from being lynched."

I didn't understand. "But it's the police who're doing us. For attempted murder and grievous bodily harm."

"They are. But don't you know the feeling this has built up? It started at your old school. That Kitchen, he's incensed with you. His supporters' club has been passing resolutions by the dozen."

"You mean the Parents' Association."

"They're scared. The more their kids take to the Boy, the more you're in danger. Have you got a gun?"

He was only half-serious. "Seriously," he said, "there's a tremendous amount of hostility to you in the town. Did you see the local news these last two evenings?"

I shook my head and went into a dazzling spin. "Did you write it?" I managed to ask.

He smiled. "I got those two cold girls, you remember, Emma and Sybil, to do it. They had Kitchen on."

I felt very lonely. My head was still spinning, my eyes ached with the room flashing round. Alistair was manipulating me far beyond my understanding. He went on: "It's an eighties thing. This decade everything is going so frighteningly wrong everywhere that people close their tiny minds until something they can touch happens and then they explode. Kitchen made a statement to the Education Committee, then gave copies to the European Union of Teachers, to the Social Welfare Department, to the press and then to Sybil's cameras. He sees you as a dangerous lunatic who's attacking the System. He didn't name Jill, and he couldn't name the Boy, but he talked about the total sexual decadence of your house. The more he talks about it, the more youngsters flock to your house. There's no grass left on the lawn. I think about a hundred kids sleep there each night. And there are many hundreds in and out of it each evening."

"What do they do?"

"Form large rings round the Boy, Mary and sometimes Christopher, and listen."

"You mean Mary talks?"

He shook his head. "They listen to themselves. It's like a disorganised Quaker meeting. Broken up occasionally when irate parents arrive to drag their kids away."

I couldn't imagine it. Alistair went on, "Sybil took her cameras there. We're going onto the National network this evening, and I'm trying hard to get onto Euro-Vision tomorrow."

"What are you doing?"

"It's perfect," he said enthusiastically, "we build this thing up into a Freedom-versus-Tyranny thing. Entice the Authorities into defending terrible Tyranny, and get youngsters everywhere to stand up, stand up for Freedom. Emma and Sybil have been waiting for something like this. It's a clear issue. In the end, the Inspector and his constable will have to admit they broke my neck and cracked your skull. We admit reasonably we attacked them but were provoked because of what we thought they were going to do to the Boy. Then we have the Boy and Mary to give evidence. By that time Sybil and Emma will have millions of young people clamouring for Freedom-and-all-that. . . ."

"What's all this about?" I asked, completely bewildered.

"I want Mary and that bloody kid of hers to be given a chance to be known everywhere by everybody. If it's true that they're the only two sane people alive today, then I want to expose them to the world."

I felt left-out, lonely, uncared-for. I had to keep my head absolutely still so I couldn't see Alistair's face as he went on: "Emma and Sybil have always been looking for a really big issue. Well, I've involved them. I've challenged them to make history around this case. Mary'll give evidence, so will the Boy. It doesn't matter what they say as long as they're seen a lot and talked about. Instead of letting history happen we're going to create it. We'll be acquitted and end up having tea with the Archbishop of Canterbury."

"After which," I managed to say, "we'll lead all the young people of England along the motorways and through the Channel Tunnel to Beauvais."

"Like two pied pipers," Alistair added gravely.

"This," I said, "is no way to plan the second coming."

"What's wrong with it?"

"We're joking all the time."

"That's where the other one went wrong."

"Which other?"

"Jesus the first . . . no sense of humour . . . I've never forgiven him for it."

"Did John the Baptist have any sense of humour?"

"No," he said, keeping his face straight, "that's why they cut off his fucking head."

We both began to laugh.

When eventually I was allowed home I found the Boy, Mary and about two hundred kids . . . not kids, young people.

Everywhere there were serious conversations going on. The kitchen was in complete chaos. Stacks of empty paper-cups, most of them used, the waste-bin piled with empty coffee-jars, and outside more piles of the same. Strangely, there was no smell of pot.

The Boy was in the garden surrounded by a group of about fifteen. Mary was walking through the hall, holding the hand of a tearful girl.

"What's wrong?" I asked the girl, in the same way I would have asked her if I'd been her headmaster. She lowered her head slightly in the direction of Mary and they passed on.

"Want some coffee, Tony?" a young voice called out. I recognised one of the freer boys from my sixth-form.

"Offering to make it?"

"Sure," he said.

I sat on the floor with the others and he got up and made for the kitchen.

"It's her parents . . . her father's forbidden her to come here. All our parents are against you," someone said.

"Why against me? All this lot don't come here to see me."

"But you started it. It's your idea."

"It's not my idea. I didn't start it . . . in fact, it's always been going on."

"But it's never happened," another said. "We're going to make it happen."

He was tall, nervous, bearded, with lustrous eyes, and long, dirty fingernails. I looked around at the group. About thirty of them.

He went on: "We're going to have a hundred thousand round the magistrate's court, a peaceful demonstration."

"We intend to plead not guilty and ask to be tried by a jury," I explained.

"Good," he said, looking across to two girls—young women—whose faces were familiar. Both wore almost identical dark suits, as if they were on their way to work in an office, white blouses and black ties. I tried to remember where I'd met them before. They came over, serious-faced, unsmiling.

"We've met," I said.

"Alistair introduced us in London. My name is Sybil Waverley and this is Emma Bedford-Smith."

They asked if they could talk. Business talk.

First of all they offered their credentials. They were organisers of demonstrations. They'd decided, as undergraduates at Oxford, to become professional in this work. Instead of working for one of the political parties, they'd gone in for pop-festivals. Sybil explained, "The first we did was about seven years ago. We got two-hundred thousand without knowing what we were doing. Logistics and sanitation were bad. And we assumed the police wouldn't cooperate. Our last was at Epsom earlier this year. Read about it?"

"No shootings," I said.

"Worked beautifully. It's got a lot to do with toilets. We want to organise something around your trial, if they have a trial."

"To make money?"

"Yes. But more than that. Our intention was originally to work up to organising huge meetings to coincide with occasions like the opening of Parliament and annual meetings of the Labour Party, but we've got this . . ."

"Why?" I interrupted.

They looked at each other, like fourth-form girls talking to a teacher. "To drown the consumer-society in oceans of timeless, simple pleasure," Emma said wondrously.

"Is this Alistair's idea or yours?"

They were very involved with each other, as if I wasn't there any more. Emma repeated, "Oceans of endless, simple pleasure." They laughed mechanically. Neither seemed warm or human. Sybil's laughter turned to a choking cough. Emma became cold. They were suddenly apart in some sense. Queer girls. The three of us were standing close to each other, but totally alone. Once more I felt helpless, out of control of what was controlling me.

I won't describe—it's common knowledge—the press and television coverage of the magistrate's court hearing. I watched one programme in the smelly remand-cells underneath the huge crowd of young people and children who were still earnestly singing above us at half-past-six in the evening. Emma and Sybil both appeared on the programme, believably warm and reasonable in front of the cameras, both arguing credibly that there was a massive attempt by the police and the local authorities to interfere with the freedom of two sensible and sensitive, responsible middle-aged men. Sybil spoke lightly of a police-conspiracy, of police-brutality, of hysteria in high educational circles, of a huge, unthinking lobby of teachers and parents who were working out their own deep fears by smearing, systematically though not very intelligently, Alistair and me, and successfully involving the police and now the legal system in their fascist-type reactionary manoeuvres. Emma thought that television and press coverage was making things worse and that the young in particular were likely to react against yet one more television campaign to blow up a local issue into a national, even international, non-event. Even so, she felt that there was evidence of collusion between the police and the local establishment. And young people, as well as the defendants in the case, were being misrepresented often by their own parents and teachers.

Bryan King appeared to report that Alistair and I had pleaded not guilty to all charges, had refused legal aid, and had been remanded in custody to the Crown Court for trial.

I don't know how many people saw Emma and Sybil's programmes. But we are so near everything that's filmable and newsworthy these days, that I think after a few days our cause—I was sure at that time, not so much now, that we had a cause though I couldn't quite get it clear in my mind—faded into the dimly-remembered frieze of the collective memory, and I think nothing much would have happened had it not been for the professional competence of Emma and Sybil. They worked thoroughly. At this stage they planned six contemporary pop-festivals, at different sites within eight miles of Leeds for the date of our trial. In the end, for logistic reasons rather than shortage of numbers, only five were held. Each was planned for a quarter of a million attendants. Their idea was to start three days before the trial, and on the fourth day, everybody was to converge on Leeds.

"We'll have two million young people in Leeds for your trial," Emma said seriously. "We'll have routes arranged and we'll control them through their transistors."

"Will they want to stay for the fourth day?" Alistair asked. We were sitting in the visitors' room at Armley Prison in Leeds.

"The way to be sure is to provide plenty of music and too many toilets. We're going to have a toilet-service that'll be the miracle of the modern age. One can for every thirty-three people, the cans being emptied and freshened continuously."

"Money?" he asked.

"We have it. We've been saving up for this. But we won't need it with numbers like that."

"Can you two control it all?" I asked.

"We've got six committees, one for each festival, and a co-ordinating committee. They're all professionals. They've all worked for us before. We've got support being offered everywhere. We're working through the Student Inter-Nation Agency, and our first train arrives the day after tomorrow."

"But it's four weeks before our trial," Alistair said.

"There's a lot of work to be done. Sites to be prepared, publicity, legal and health work, insurance work . . . you'd be amazed how much has to be done to be sure that things happen as one intends."

There was a long silence.

Eventually I said: "It's quite clear that this is all nothing to do with me."

Alistair looked at me, smiling.

"You're both being taken on by events you don't comprehend," Sybil stated.

"Who does?" I asked.

"The Boy doesn't," Sybil replied, "but Mary does."

"The Boy will," Alistair added. "He's the one who'll march on over our graves."

"There'll be no marching," Emma said with feeling. "Strolling happily, timelessly, yes. Marching, no."

"Marching or not," Sybil articulated, "nothing will ever be the same after this."

As we talked, Sybil switched on the television news service.

The news-studio was in total, visible disarray.

We quickly gathered that with the same unpredictable aggression the Japanese had shown the world at Pearl Harbour, the South African Army had simultaneously attacked Zambia and Tanzania, using what the Official South African World Press release called "clean tactical laser-nuclear devices of low megaton calibre."

The release described the 'communist preparations', long known to the South African Government for military attack by the Black Africa Freedom Army upon South Africa.

Film was shown of what appeared to be Black Africa military organisations in an advanced state of readiness. Assurances were given to the rest of the world that the South African Government were interested in defending their country, World Peace, and the rights of the people in all nations to control their own future. . .

"Damn," said Sybil.

You must remember how the whole world was stunned. My memory is of television stations everywhere transmitting news twenty-four hours a day. The United Nations Organisation was in full session daily. The city-fighting in America stopped completely, started again in earnest for a day or two, then slackened perhaps because of the absence of interest shown by the news media. Strikes were settled. Organised masses of blacks in the Senate lobbied for the Black Africa Freedom Army.

Each country prepared its armed and civil forces against the possibility of fuller nuclear exchanges. Panics for this and that—food, building materials for fall-out shelters, fuel—were endless in every part of the world. Leaders of Organised Religion were constantly appearing on Television alternating between appeals for world-wide commonsense, and denouncing Governments while announcing the millennium.

I had been hoping that our little circumstances might be overlooked. Unfortunately, as it turned out, the British Government, taking a stern view of all civil unrest at a time of national and international crisis, decided to continue with the trial and use the events to demonstrate Her Majesty's determination to enforce law and order.

"Thank God," Emma said a day or two before the trial, "that South Africa did it weeks ago. If it had happened today there'd 've been nobody here at all." She'd told us that the numbers at the pop-festivals, coupled with those already in the city, were going to add up to well over two millions.

"Will you be able to control them?" I asked Emma and Sybil several times. Emma was always confident. Sybil seemed to be less concerned with control problems, and more concerned with publicity. It appeared that there would be world coverage of a sparse nature.

"We need two sets of quins or an epidemic of bubonic plague to get the coverage I want."

"Or a riot," Alistair put in quietly.

"Just another riot wouldn't do it," Emma said. "Nothing short of all-out war between us and the police would attract the least bit of attention."

"I think you're right, Emma," Sybil said.

That night I lay in my cell thinking seriously about my part in the Alistair–Emma–Sybil plan. I felt responsible for triggering what I half-knew could be a catastrophe. I was surprised to find that, quite calmly, I wondered whether I ought to go on living.

The day before the trial I spent time with my kids. They were allowed to stay for over two hours. They were subdued. We watched on the telly the South African delegates at the United Nations repeating what had always been their official propaganda, that only three tactical laser-nuclear devices of low calibre had been exploded, and that each had been 'clean' as the rest of the world could now confirm in light of the fact that fall-out had been raised, on average, by only a tiny fraction and would remain well below those reached after the Americans had exploded their devices in 1945.

Three spoke in turn, each giving reassurances, each commending those Western Governments that had taken a broad view of the incidents, repeating that the incidents were defensive only, that every attempt was being made by South Africa as well as the United Nations, to offer to the stricken African Nations all the help possible to repair the terrible damage and replace the Evil Governments that had called upon themselves and the brave decent African peoples the nuclear assault.

The last one to speak had a special word for France who had

been the most understanding of the World's Nations, and was a model to all the Western World for its political and diplomatic maturity. I'd noticed myself that France had been the least disturbed, as a nation, by the events in Africa. Also, I learned from Emma and Sybil, there was only moderate interest among the French in the events in Leeds.

"What do you think?" I asked the kids after we'd turned off the telly.

"It's all balls," Michael said.

Annie said, "I think it's the end of the world starting."

John, who had been looking round a good deal since he had been brought into the prison, said: "I thought people came to prison to be punished."

Leeds was still an orderly city on the morning of our hearing.

By ten in the morning, one-and-a-half-million young people from every country in Europe were reported to be in the city. Another half-a-million or so were approaching it. The streets, for the six miles from Armley Prison to the Assize Court in the centre of the city, were filled with well-behaved youngsters, mostly listening to their wirelesses by means of which Sybil, using the Leeds City Radio Station's transmitter, spoke to them continuously. Soldiers and police seemed to be everywhere, though I gathered this was true only of the roads from the prison to the Assizes, and in the immediate vicinity of the Court.

Helicopters—civil, military and 'televisual'—were much in evidence.

The Court itself was surrounded by large numbers of soldiers. I saw the insignia of two Guards Regiments as well as—this may have been the cardinal mistake—an Irish Regiment.

Within the cordons of soldiers were many covered vehicles inside of which one glimpsed the usual appurtenances of crowd control. They also contained, as was discovered later, medium and heavy machine guns. The Chief Constable of Leeds, who was the controller of the forces of Law and Order, was talking to the crowds pressing against the cordon. He had a loudspeaker system that was ludicrously inadequate. In the end, it was Sybil who commanded the day. And I suppose if she had lived she would have claimed that she won it.

I remember feeling very overwhelmed and depressed. I heard the cheering start as Alistair and I got out of our cars—we'd been accorded the privilege of separate cars—but I didn't connect it at all with what I felt I was going through. Alistair, his face set in a peculiar way, turned and raised his handcuffs over his head. At a given signal, the huge crowds all turned their wirelesses to full volume, and their cheers were replaced by an ageing John Lennon singing, of all things, "Mother . . . you had me but I never had you." I wanted to laugh out loud with Alistair but he was not listening to the huge noise nor was he looking at me. He was staring at the top of the Courthouse steps up which we were being led. In a little group, consisting of Mary, the Boy, and Anthony Johnson, was a man I hadn't seen before. He was obviously Alistair's brother, Donald, the family resemblance was clear, but he was dressed in mourning: black morning suit, white shirt with starched collar, grey top hat, and black patent-leather shoes.

He was strongly-built though not as tall or broad as Alistair, with the same bent, powerful shoulders, long, very-grey hair. Alistair's guards, young policemen, hesitated to let Alistair speak with him.

He said to Alistair: "I've been searched for concealed weapons and . . ."

"It's bloody nice of you to come, Donald. Here, meet my fellow criminal."

Donald and I shook hands as well as we could. Donald looked over my shoulder at the soldiers and the crowds, then asked if I understood what was going on.

I shook my head. He said: "Our Alistair doesn't, either."

I looked from Donald to Alistair, and then to the Johnson family. Anthony came forward and put his arms round me then round Alistair, though they hadn't been introduced.

"It's the end of the old order," Anthony said, "I've waited a long time to see this morning."

Both Alistair and I stared at him. I said to him, viciously, "You mean that you've planned all this?"

"Nay, not me," he said, "but I started something very big and then waited for it to grow and to surprise me with the way it grew. Look at her . . ."

He indicated Mary.

She was totally alert: all-alert to everything that was happening.

She turned to us: "There's a long way to go," she said, pronouncing each word distinctly and stiffly, "but we are about the mother's business."

That's what she said. I remember it clearly.

Then, at my side, I heard Donald and Alistair speak:

"I'll stay in court if you don't mind," Donald said.

"You're dressed for it. I'm right glad you came."

"I like the Boy and his family."

"You mean you want into this thing?"

Donald shook his head: "I didn't say that."

"I hope I can do my stuff."

"What are you going to do?"

"Simply put Mary and the Boy on the stand."

"Is that so sensational?"

"The opposite. Simple chilling honesty . . . the Boy will blow the whole fucking process up with dignified truth . . . simple truth."

"Alistair likes to exaggerate," Donald said to me, smiling. Then to Alistair: "It won't be in there that things are blown up."

As Alistair and I disappeared from view there was a great roar from the crowd, and thousands broke through. Many people afterwards said it was planned. We were hurried down and locked in a cell.

"I've been here before," Alistair said.

I swung round. I had to steady myself until the dizziness passed away.

"These cells, you mean?"

He nodded.

It was early afternoon before we were led up to the dock.

We had been vaguely informed that there was trouble outside, but when we emerged into the dock, escorted by two policemen, the noise outside was deafening.

Gradually my ears became attuned to it: a mixture of loud music, admonitions over the tannoy from the Chief Constable, jeering, cheering and shrieking from the crowd, and the occasional explosion. The Court itself was empty except for the Judge—a woman—the officials, the Jury, the lawyers, several policemen acting as ushers, and Anthony Johnson with Donald in the public gallery.

We had a word with the Prosecuting Counsel just before coming up and we'd agreed to plead not-guilty to the charges, but not to dispute the facts of the assault, only their interpretation.

Very quickly the Judge, scarlet-faced, dry, shrewd, asked us to reconsider whether we should be represented by counsel. She had arranged for one to be available should we so wish it, and although she was anxious to hear the case—it was in all our interests as well as the interests of those outside that there should be no delay—she was quite prepared to adjourn the court for a period to allow us to brief a counsel. We declined. The Judge then instructed the Jury—my impression is that they took little part in the trial and were among the most apprehensive in the Court when the shooting started outside—that she was prepared, and so should they be, to sit until the case was heard and their verdict reached.

They nodded in quick agreement.

"We're on our way," Alistair whispered as the wigged prosecuting counsel stood up and addressed the Jury.

He outlined the surprise attack by two—articulated heavily: 'apparently responsible men' on an Inspector and a Constable going about their lawful duty. Before calling witnesses to show the grievousness of the attack, he wished to emphasise to the Jury that it was unusual for defendants to appear without counsel. He felt this ploy of the defendants was not unconnected with the organised mass demonstration outside the court, which they could all hear. He trusted that if the defendants hoped to attract sympathy from the Jury by being unrepresented, or if they wished to exert pressure on the Jury by massive demonstrations, then he had every confidence that the Jury would pay attention only to the evidence because he, the prosecuting counsel, had an easy task: the evidence in the case was clear and he would do no more than present it for their consideration. He said that the whole world could blow up but British Justice and a British Court of Law could not be deflected from its duty.

He reminded them of the events in America, Russia and other countries where enforcement of Law and Order had become a matter of fierce and bloody fighting. He mentioned the long campaign in Northern Ireland and the chaos that ensued when Law and Order were not enforced. He went on to point out the importance, here in a country that was relatively peaceful, of protecting the police from aggression. The aggression in this case had been considerable, he said, and he called medical witnesses who testified to the damage to each of the two policemen. The Inspector was the more damaged.

Both policemen appeared in turn, giving identical descriptions of the attack, but each glossing over the circumstances of their presence in my house. Their descriptions were fair, much duller than the incident they were describing, and both produced a word-for-word affirmation that they had retaliated, in self-defence, using the minimum force to allow them to carry out their lawful duties.

After each witness we were asked if we had any questions.

Alistair, answering for both of us, said that we had none, but reserved the right to recall the two policemen. The Counsel then finished his plea by explaining that in spite of the million or two young people in the town outside, there was nothing of major importance at stake other than the principle that the police should be protected from aggression.

The Judge and Jury were bored when Alistair started our defence. He began: "Your Honour, I think and speak better when I walk about. The Prosecuting Counsel was able to wander about. May I exercise the same freedom?"

She nodded, saying: "Feel free to walk about but not, at least until the Jury has arrived at a verdict, out of my Court." She was pleased with her humour, as were the Jury.

Shots were fired outside the Court. There was an instant buzz of conversations which the Judge firmly quietened, saying we were obliged to carry on with our business.

Alistair walked stiffly down into the Court, exaggerating the restrictions placed upon him by his plastic neck-collar.

"I rely upon you, your Honour," he said, "to keep me inside the necessary protocols of this court."

She nodded, adding: "No doubt I will be ably assisted by my legal colleague sitting opposite you."

Alistair turned to stare at Prosecuting Counsel. Then he turned back to the Judge to request that 'our' two Policemen be brought to sit in court. She doubted the wisdom of this. Alistair insisted. They were duly ushered in.

The Judge then asked: "Have you at last arranged my court to your satisfaction?"

Alistair smiled nervously, glancing round with jerky, furtive movements within his plastic collar.

"I don't intend, Ladies and Gentlemen," he said to the Jury, "to bore you with painful medical refutations about how bad were the injuries Mr Foster and I inflicted on the two policemen.

Indeed, they have my sympathy, Mr Foster's also, and quite properly yours. Both Mr Foster and I deeply regret our part in the fight.

"Nor will I add to your discomfort and general boredom by calling medical evidence to describe how damaged we both were after what has been called the 'minimal force' used by these two gentlemen." He nodded towards the two policemen. "Enough to say they gave rather better than they got. My neck, or a small bone in it was broken, and Mr Foster suffered temporary brain damage. He was unconscious for two days. One of the results of the damage to his brain is he now uses words rather better than before, but no doubt this is temporary . . ."

No-one laughed.

". . . he doesn't understand them any better than he did, but at least the knock on the head did him good as well as harm." I noticed broad smiles now in the Jury.

"I think, Mr . . ." the Judge glanced down to her papers, ". . . Shuttleworth, you've established that point, if you would like to continue . . ."

The Counsel for the prosecution was watching Alistair's effect on the Jury.

"That apart," Alistair went on, bowing slightly to the Judge, "I would like to draw your attention to the fact that there were witnesses to this incident."

He paused, turning back to look at the two policemen, then back to the prosecuting Counsel.

The Jury were very interested, suddenly, and followed his glances. He went on: "The two policemen chose to leave out this significant fact because they believed that we would not wish to disclose these witnesses."

The Counsel jumped up and said that so far as he could see there was an agreement between Prosecution and Defence that there was to be no dispute as to the incidents, in which case, witnesses were not material to the case. He went on:

"Indeed, Your Honour, Mr Shuttleworth may be well advised that it is not in his interest . . . definitely not in his interest to call these witnesses, who, I understand, are eccentric, to say the least, in their personal habits."

"Well, Mr Shuttleworth," the Judge asked, "are these witnesses able to add anything relevant to these events which you have agreed did happen substantially as the two police officers have described to us?"

"Yes, Madam," Alistair said.

"So far, apart from rather amusing aplomb, you've failed to say anything that supports the case of you and the co-defendant. I trust it is your intention to say something or get others to say something that will have that effect, otherwise, you're wasting the time of everyone here."

"My case, Madam, is that one of these two police officers attacked a Boy of eleven who I wish to call, and that Mr Foster and I defended that Boy, who we both feel is rather special, from attack with the same mistaken zeal and passion with which the officers then defended themselves from us."

The Judge looked undecided. Alistair continued:

"There are unusual and relevant facts that the Jury need to know, and this rather special Boy and his mother can provide those facts."

"It's terribly difficult to know what weight to allow the testimony of a minor. Is he intelligent?"

Alistair nodded.

"Call him," she said.

She looked to the Counsel who just noticeably, as if they colluded, shook his head wearily, meaning 'we're wasting our time."

"Thank you, Madam. May I just mention to the Jury that this Boy is unusually beautiful of personality . . ."

Counsel stood up, indicating he wanted to speak.

"I would like to ask Mr Shuttleworth if the boy also has two heads and whether . . ." The Court cracked out laughing. Counsel waited: ". . . and whether his mother is the fattest lady in the world."

More laughter. Alistair, agitated, walked about the court,

impatient to speak. Once the laughter subsided: "The Jury must decide for themselves whether they are being addressed by a freak. Will someone ask for Jesus Johnson?"

Everyone laughed again. The laughter was drowned by the heavy repetitive firing of machine guns. Shrieks, screams, rumbling of tanks. The Judge was very concerned. The Court was silent. Deeply apprehensive. The Police Inspector stood up. The Judge looked to her officers in the court.

It seemed that the trial would be interrupted.

The Boy appeared. He seemed taller. He was dressed in white trousers, very short and beautifully cut, and a white blouse, open at the neck. His body was brown. His long, slender legs were bare as were his feet. He stood looking round the court. Impressive, self-contained, he walked forward. There was absolute silence in the Court in spite of the continuing gunfire outside. His manner was relaxed and magnificently controlled as he looked about him. He saw me and smiled a warm, full smile. Then he turned to the Judge, waiting to be asked questions. He was handed the oath but the Judge indicated that it was unnecessary and instead explained to him that he must take great care to tell the truth. He nodded seriously, turning to glance at Alistair. The Clerk asked him to state his name.

"I have no name other than the name of the woman you would call my mother. She is Mary Johnson, and I am thinking of using the name 'Jesus'." He spoke carefully, looking at the Clerk. "So I may be known for a bit as Jesus Johnson."

There was a tiny, short-lived splutter of laughter. The Judge asked him if this woman, Mary Johnson, was in court.

"Yes, Madam," he said.

"Do you know why she didn't give you a name?"

"I think she wanted me to choose my own." There was another splutter of laughter.

"How do you know who you are?"

"I don't find it a problem, Madam, but I know others do sometimes."

"Why are you thinking of using the name Jesus?"

"It started as a joke." He had said that sadly and somehow stoically. No-one spoke for a time. Sporadic shots outside the court punctuated the silence. Alistair waited, then, very quietly, asked him to tell the Jury what happened when the policemen came to see him. The Boy walked over to the Jury to face them. This the Prosecuting Counsel objected to, but his objection was waived by the Judge. The Boy walked in front of the Jury, looking at each in turn, as he spoke: "Tony, Mr Foster, told me that two policemen were coming to ask which bed I slept in. I was called into the sitting room and there they all were." He glanced at the two policemen, then at Alistair and me.

The Judge leaned forward: "And where did you sleep?"

"With Mr Foster."

"In his bed?"

"Yes."

Silence.

Alistair asked him to continue.

"They asked me my name, and we had the usual difficulties . . ." He smiled. The Judge was reserved. The Jury were interested. "And then they asked me where I lived and I told them in France with Mary who they would call my mother but is really a lot of people, and Christopher, who is not my father. I told them that the three of us sleep together in France. This made the Inspector very angry and he wished to hit me. He was unable to speak, he was so angry . . . frightened in a way. He raised his hand to smack me. Then Mr Shuttleworth attacked him, Mr Foster attacked the other policeman who was going to help the other . . . then . . ."

The Judge stopped him.

"Just a minute . . ." She was unable to articulate the word 'Jesus'. "I'd like to get this exactly right. The Inspector raised his hand?"

"He raised his hand to strike me across the head. Alistair attacked him. Then Tony attacked the second policeman who was going to help the first. They were all very angry."

She asked him what he meant.

"The Inspector, and the other policeman also, looked angrily at each other. They didn't want to know about how Mary, Christopher and I live. I think they felt that there is something very wrong in the way we live. I can understand that now after talking to English children."

"Did the Inspector ask you whether you slept in the same bed as that gentleman over there, Mr Foster?"

"No. The fighting started then and there were no more questions."

"You think, then, that the Inspector started it?"

"No," he said, "I started it by telling how we live in Beauvais."

"But you were asked that?"

"Not really. I thought he wanted to ask about where I slept so I told him before he asked. I think that was bad . . . for me to tell him, but I think that he would have become angry anyway."

Silence.

Alistair indicated that he wanted to ask nothing more.

The Judge spoke to the Counsel:

"I've already asked a number of questions that might have been more properly asked by you, but it is unusual to have such an intelligent and straightforward boy in a hearing such as this. I suggest that you are most circumspect in any attempt you may wish to make to discredit his evidence."

The Counsel nodded as the Judge spoke. Then he turned to the Boy.

"How old are you?"

"Eleven."

"Goodness, I would have thought you were fourteen or fifteen. Do you go to school?"

"Only to see what they do."

Laughter.

"So who educates you?"

"I do it mainly myself, but I get a lot of help from Mary and the others . . . there's Christopher, of course, and Anthony, Mary's father. Oh, and Roger when he visits."

"And who is Roger?"

"He is a retired Anglican bishop."

The Counsel was off balance. "So you educate yourself but get help from these others. I see. Do you teach yourself mathematics, for example?"

"I mainly unlearn things. I'm not interested in mathematics."

"Oh, I see. Well, what are you interested in?"

"At the moment, in reading. I started to learn to read only a few months ago and I'm reading rather a lot."

"You live in France, but I take it you mean in English?"

"Well, I'm learning to read French, German and Spanish at the same time as English. It's easier that way."

The Counsel thought he was being taken in. He spoke in slow German to the Boy who answered at length in German. The Judge smiled: "I take it," she said to the Counsel, "that you are not very fluent in German but I can tell you that the witness speaks it fluently, accurately, even elegantly."

There was a good deal of restlessness in Court, most people being bored, I think. The Counsel floundered on:

"I see. You speak several languages and you're learning to read them now. Making much progress?"

The Boy nodded.

"You said that you mainly unlearn things. What does that mean?"

"Well, if you take a word even . . . a word like 'boy' . . . it is a lot of sort of instructions for how one person thinks about and behaves with another. It stops me knowing myself a bit when other people think of me as a boy . . . instead of a person. It stops them knowing me a bit as well. So I concentrate on sort of unlearning what words mean so that I don't miss any of what I mean to myself and to others."

The Judge had stopped writing. She looked closely at him, leaning forward and taking off her spectacles. She asked, "So you want to know yourself better and to do that you unlearn meanings."

He nodded, looking directly into her face.

"It's all inside me, between me and other people, and inside them. Words and thinking in words sort of changes it all."

"And it's to do with words."

"In the beginning it isn't, but once words start, then things are changed by the words . . . sometimes made better, sometimes worse."

He stood thinking for some time. Everyone in the Court was waiting for what he had to say.

"Words miss who I am . . . go round reality."

"There is a reality and what people call you avoids it?" she said.

"The reality is a lot of things happening at the same time . . . changing and changing . . . and words make it all seem to stand still."

"So it's all to do with words?"

"It's to do with learning all the things that you really know but are hidden from you . . . all the inside things I mean."

"Don't those who live with you treat you as a boy?"

"No . . . I think Roger always does but he doesn't come often and I don't mind. Christopher when he's unhappy . . . Mary never has, I think. And Anthony never has."

"What about the two defendants . . . Mr Shuttleworth and Mr Foster?"

"I only sleep with Mr Foster."

The Court laughed.

The Judge smiled, adjusted herself in her seat, and waited for the laughter to die down. Then she said: "Not all grown ups want to know who you sleep with."

He listened to her, bowing slightly, his head to one side.

She went on: "I was asking if these two gentlemen treat you as a boy."

"Oh, they try to, very hard sometimes, but they find it a bit difficult."

Silence.

The Judge wrote more notes, then she looked across at the Counsel. He gestured faintly. She said: "Well, if Mr Shuttleworth has nothing more to put to you, you may go now. Thank you for being so clear."

He looked at her, then at Alistair, then at me. The usher gently led him from the witness box and out of the court.

Alistair was reluctant to break the silence that followed his exit. He waited until the first mutterings in the court reached the jury before he called Mary.

There were some fierce whispers as she walked forward wearing a light coat, and was sworn in.

The Judge asked her if she believed in God.

"I believe in the word God," Mary answered.

"And that was your son who has just . . . entertained us with a little lucid thinking?"

"He's far more than a son."

"But he's not your daughter?" the Judge asked sharply.

"Neither he nor I think in those terms. At times he is my daughter. He has well-developed aspects of his personality that you might experience as feminine."

"I see," said the Judge, irritated by Mary's manner more than her insistence. Mary took off her overcoat. She was wearing a loose white see-through dress, short, no support to her strong breasts, no make-up or jewellery. Her body was brown.

Alistair asked her to describe the incident.

She said that she came in just before the fighting started. She described the events clearly. Alistair asked her to account for the events.

Mary turned to the Jury and said: "It is beyond doubt that the Inspector intended to strike the Boy . . ."

The Judge cut in: "Did you do anything yourself to stop him?"

"No, madam. I was too far away to interpose my body between the Inspector and the Boy."

"Did you feel aggressive yourself?"

"No, madam."

"What makes you think the Inspector intended to strike your son?"

"He was in the process of striking him. And his anger was such that he was out of control of his aggression."

"Can you be sure?"

"I am sure."

"Beyond all reasonable doubt?"

"Sure."

"You mean 'yes'."

"Yes, madam."

"Can you account for the anger of the Inspector?"

"Not accurately. But I think each of the four men was out of control for similar reasons."

Mary stopped, listening to again what I can only call inner voices. She looked beautiful.

The firing outside had been intermittent. At this point there was a barrage of shots, the rumble and squeal again of tanks moving over concrete, many terrible screams.

The shooting stopped suddenly.

A Superintendent of Police, his face cut and bleeding badly, came into the court, looked around, and with a resigned gesture begged leave to speak to the Judge, who beckoned him forward.

They whispered together. She looked across at the two policemen, then to Alistair: "Do you wish to question these police officers?"

He shook his head. The two policemen stood up. She whispered briefly to the Superintendent who went out and his two colleagues followed. The Judge said:

"There is considerable disorder outside, and much loss of life, but I am determined that we continue with our business." To Mary: "Please continue."

"I think all four men have been shamed, as infants, out of their innocence. I think, coerced into denying many of their feelings. To be in opposition, two against two, in the presence of a free and innocent Boy made each of them intensely anxious . . . agitated may be a better word. All four are men who deal with anxiety by being aggressive."

The Counsel stood up and asked if Mary was a qualified psychologist.

"I read a degree, here in Leeds, in Psychology, but the accuracy of what I'm saying doesn't depend on my training." Sarcastic, he asked: "Would you be good enough to tell the Jury, who are not psychologists, why you feel you understand what happened between these four men?"

"The simple answer is that I do not share their inhibitions and neuroticisms, so their behaviour is clear to me."

"And you expect the members of the Jury to take your word for that?"

"They must judge for themselves."

"And that's precisely what I have every confidence they will do," he said heavily.

"You patronise them," Mary said.

He was very angry. He became white, hesitating, wanting to speak harsh words.

"Do you wish to say something?" the Judge asked him.

"I'm too angry to speak coherently, Madam."

"Then pray sit down, sir," she said. She was very thoughtful. She turned to Mary: "Let me get your testimony clear in my mind. You say you are a trained psychologist but that your opinions don't rest on your professional knowledge. You believe that these four men, all four, were out of control for similar reasons, namely that their own denial of what you choose to call their innocence was exposed. Then why did they fight? Why didn't they turn, all four, on the Boy?"

"Because each deals with his denials differently. The defendants wish, have long wished, to deny their denials . . . to regain their innocence . . . to re-occupy the innocent but repressed parts of their personality. The two police officers wish to affirm their denials."

Mary waited until the Judge had finished writing.

Then the Judge: "You're suggesting—I think I ought to make this clear for the benefit of the Jury—that there is some degree of repressed homosexuality in each of the four men."

Before allowing Mary to answer, she said to the Jury:

"May I remind you that the Prosecuting Counsel is absolutely correct in what he said to you: You must judge for yourself what value to put upon the testimony of this witness."

The Judge looked to Mary, who turned to face the Jury: "Not only repressed homosexuality . . . but all the repressed truth of them . . . all the repressed love of the person they were, as little children, shamed from being. If they have children, the repressions that prevented them from fully expressing their feelings for their own children. I refer to a complex process of cultural repression that has its roots in the way children in this country, in Europe, perhaps in Western Society, have been brought up historically and the meaning that has come to be attached to the way children are experienced by their parents and so come to experience themselves."

The Judge wrote on. Then: "I take it you have brought up your child in what might be called culture-free circumstances?"

Mary assented.

"What you've said to us is in fact a deep and damning criticism of our culture."

"A criticism that is being made every day by many people," Mary answered.

"But still, if everyone thought like you then society as we have come to know it would disappear," the Judge persisted.

Mary didn't answer.

In the distance fresh outbursts of firing could be heard. The Judge sat, her head to one side, looking up at the ceiling.

The Court became restless. One or two of the Jury were extremely frightened and it was clear from their gestures they wanted to get out of the court.

The Judge, looking across at Mary, then to Alistair, wrote something down and called the Counsel and Alistair forward.

I gather she said that the charges against us were unnecessarily severe and she felt it was her duty to direct the Jury to return a verdict of not-guilty, and that if the prosecution agreed to this, and if we were so prepared, then she thought that the lesser charge of Obstructing the Police might be more appropriate. If we would plead guilty to this lesser charge we could rely on her discretion and the whole thing would be ended.

Shortly after Alistair and I had been bound over to keep the peace, the police Superintendent came in and asked that the court be cleared quickly as they wished to use it. I joined Anthony, and his brother Donald, at the entrance to the court.

Outside was strangely quiet. None of us was quite prepared for what we saw.

Ambulances were beginning to arrive. It was not possible to count the number of dead, many of them soldiers. I don't think that any of the subsequent televisual coverage over-stated the extent of what was really a mutual massacre.

Emma still believes that most of the crowd got guns from fallen soldiers. But it had been common knowledge that the police, who had searched the crowds as they arrived for the Festival, had failed to find most of the guns that students and young people now normally carry when they move about Europe.

There were bodies, many grotesquely still, others moving in slow pain, or convulsing, in private trauma.

It looked as if the battle had started round the Courthouse, with, judging from the number of dead and wounded and the way they were strewn about, heavy firing from both sides. Then the crowd, at least the armed elements, must have withdrawn under heavy fire, the soldiers following. Much has been made of the apparent disregard for life on both sides. John Lennon in his interview in 'The Times' said that it was as if neither side wanted to live. The Chief Constable of Leeds, you may remember, told one television reporter that "the heroism of soldiers and police may have been equalled in the civil history of this country, but has never been surpassed." Conversely, Emma talked about "young idealists strolling happily into death in a final, beautiful assertion of revolutionary insight." Many of the dead were singing as they fell. "Death was different," Emma said. It was she who had persuaded Sybil to leave the studio at Leeds City Radio Centre to do an 'inspection of the front'. It was Emma who had been left standing when a burst of heavy machine-gun fire had knocked down everybody around her. Sybil's body had been torn open. "Almost no blood," Emma had told Alistair.

The film of Mary and the Boy walking from the Courthouse—they came out before the rest of us—is difficult to describe. I've seen it several times at private showings but it hasn't yet been released for public showing. If it is ever networked—Alistair intends to use it extensively when he gets his UNESCO programmes going—it might stop the world, if only for a careless second.

Mary is carrying her coat so that the strong sun shines through her dress, outlining the free movements of her body as if she's naked. The Boy holds her hand. They walk among the dead and dying, bending, kneeling to hold those in pain or needing assurance. Moving into the square are many soldiers and increasing numbers of medical workers and ambulance-crews. In the distance a fresh outburst of explosions, an irregular sequence of massive bumps juddering the ground, is followed by much shooting.

In the square those moving in to help become aware of Mary and the Boy. Her strength, her charisma, the force of her feelings and her movements, attract the attention of everyone, so for a moment she and the Boy move among the dead and dying within a very wide circle of spectators. Some of the wounded painfully shift their damaged bodies to watch. The Boy, suddenly looking up and around him, fails to understand the quiet onlookers, and turns to attract Mary's attention. His feelings bulge ominously, forcing his body into stiff, twitching gestures. He weeps, his eyes open. He looks searchingly into Mary's eyes. His body shivers. He looks around at the carnage, then at the onlookers, then back into Mary's eyes.

Mary leans down and kisses him on his lips, then turns as a young man, wearing pastel-coloured clothes brown-stained with blood shouts out in pain. He holds candle-white intestines which tumble and twist out of the savage lips of a gaping body-wound. Mary kneels down to him, taking his hand. He speaks to her, nodding feebly towards the Boy:

"That Boy shouldn't be here," he whispers.

Mary looks across to the crew of a heli-ambulance. They come to life, take a stretcher off their vehicle and hurry towards her. The Boy watches, his shoulders shuddering tinily as he cries, his face collapsed.

Again the young man whispers to Mary who turns, looks into the Boy's face until he controls his weeping, then turns and moves to the next wounded, a soldier with his throat and face badly gashed. His hands are cupped about his throat. When he takes his hands away, his throat jets a stream of crimson blood onto Mary's face and dress. She presses one hand firmly on the gash, calling the Boy over with a gesture. He kneels down with her.

The thought of touching the dead always has been repulsive to me, but I found myself, along with Alistair, Donald—still in his mourning clothes—and the army of soldiers and policemen, working through the bodies, helping those alive, covering, then carrying those beyond help. Later, a large number of young people came back to join in the gruesome work. It was the early hours of the morning before Anthony collected Mary, Jesus, Alistair, his brother and me to take us back to Jane Johnson's to eat and sleep. Mary and Jesus went straight to bed. Christopher and Jane had followed the grievous events of the day on Television, and were in deep shock. They sat about unresponsive to attempts to relieve them.

We sat out in the cool night air, moodily preoccupied with what had happened. There was no remorse, nor feelings of guilt in Alistair's episodic account of the day. Christopher didn't speak. Anthony, I felt, was disgustingly complacent, somehow implicating himself with the authorship of everything that had happened, at the same time dismissing any individual's contribution. He spoke of truth—a Woman—so long violated by the circumstances of contemporary society, emerging like the God of the Old Testament, to establish Herself again. When Emma arrived to tell us that Sybil was dead, she was ecstatic. All those corpses were a testament to the rebirth of the beautiful life and the Age of the Mother.

I left them to their macabre conversations and went into the old Church. I sat there, half-asleep, until it got light. Christopher came in, followed by others. We waited for the sun to light up the window. When it did there was a general feeling of disappointment. I personally felt nothing for the window. I felt, for anyone who wanted to know, that as a group we were way-out, silly, dangerous—very dangerous—and uninformed.

Alistair and Emma, professionally keen to exploit the events surrounding us, arranged for Mary to be interviewed two days later. Bryan King was persuaded to do it and the idea was to use the old Church as a back-cloth.

"Will this one be shown?" Mary asked Alistair. He shrugged his shoulders.

She began by saying in answer to a question about the Leeds massacre, that it was a massacre of the innocents. Bryan King asked: "You mean, Miss Johnson, that you believe the young pop-people were innocent?" Mary shook her head:

"There were many young soldiers killed and wounded also," she said.

"What was your part in that massacre?"

"I am attracting men and women around me who feel the need to change society radically and immediately."

"Does this worry you?"

"No."

"You feel partly responsible for the massacre and yet you aren't worried?"

"Not worried. I feel for those involved, and those who loved those involved. But 'worry' is not among my feelings."

"What is it," Bryan asked, "that attracts these men and women to you?"

"I believe they find in me a transcendence that appeals to them. And in those I live with."

"The Boy?"

"I live with my father, my husband, though we are not married, and my son, though we try to avoid, not always successfully, the stereotyped roles of traditional family life."

They were now strolling into the church.

Cameras were back-tracking along the aisle, followed by Mary and Bryan: "You used the word 'transcendence'. Can you tell us what it is?"

"Not on television . . . not anywhere. Transcendence can only be lived."

"Would it be true to say that you want to be a revelation?" He spoke cynically.

They were approaching the Blake window. I think Mary wanted to answer standing in front of the Mother and Child. She ignored Bryan, and looked straight in the camera,

"The revelation that I am concerned with will start—will be initiated—when parents lovingly give up their children to knowledge, and children find themselves able and willing to give up their parents to knowledge."

"What knowledge?"

"Knowledge to urge what we perceive beyond the limits of its delusive completeness, and at the same time, to urge the prejudices of science beyond their delusive air of finality. I am quoting a thinker called Whitehead."

"I don't think many people will understand what you're saying . . . I don't for one. Can you explain more simply?"

"So far as revelation is concerned, simple explanations are bogus. Perhaps a simpler way of putting it is that the knowledge that we are discussing is of what is changeless among all that changes . . . that's no better. I wish I knew a simple way to define what you ask about. In this matter any simplification is over-simplification."

There was a quality about Mary in that church that was surely not filmable. Outside the Courthouse, not only because of what

Emma recently called 'marvellous props'—she meant the sun, Mary's apparent nakedness as well as the carnage of bodies and the Boy—but also because the reactions of others to her were visible, the film of her works, shows her as she is. I haven't seen the film of this interview yet, and both Alistair and Bryan who have, think it works also, but I can't imagine it. I can't believe they've got her as, to me, she always seemed—seems—connected with everything and everybody around her. On this occasion I watched her move to touch the worn oak of the lectern. She was absorbing the church and being absorbed by it. She was complete whether Bryan asked her another question or not.

"Recently you spoke of Western European society disappearing, of profound changes, now you speak of revelation. Is it your wish to be the fairy godmother of a new European Society?"

"I wish to be what I am."

"But as you admit, without you there would've been no massacre of what you chose to call 'the innocents'."

"But I am here. I wish to be wherever I am."

"I see. You wish to be what you are, wherever you are. That's your message, is it, Mary Johnson?"

Mary looked at Bryan steadily. He turned to the director:

"Can we cut for a minute?"

Bryan King lit a cigarette. "As you see, Miss Johnson, I'm not sympathetic enough for you."

"Your questions don't matter. That you ask here in this church is enough."

"And your answers don't matter?" he asked.

"My answers are less important than my life . . . my living. It matters that I'm here. With you . . . your being here is important."

She smiled. Bryan studied her face. Very angry. I thought at that moment he was near to striking her.

That evening—the filming continued in the flood-lit churchyard—I noticed David and Christopher striding towards the village, skirting the vans and equipment of the television crews.

"I didn't realise that David was here," I said to Anthony.

"Christopher invited him . . . he rang up, Christopher answered and asked him here."

"It's strange how the two of them get on." We were sitting in front of a coal fire in Jane's huge living room.

"They're both innocents."

"But what about David's eyes? They're cold. They frighten me at times."

"Oh . . . I find them warm, friendly," Anthony said, shifting on his chair to be more comfortable. Jane brought in coffee while he spoke. I was nonplussed. "They're so bloody innocent, both of them, that one could think of them as emotional murderees . . . they attract violence."

"In which case I'm a murderer," I heard myself say.

"I am of men," Anthony said, "but not of women. That's right, isn't it love?" He took Jane's hand as she put a cup of coffee next to him.

"I don't know what you're talking about," she said.

"Life," Anthony announced, waving his arms exuberantly. "It's men killing the bad in men, in themselves, letting the good find itself, multiply and enjoy its fullness."

"The trouble with men," Jane retorted, looking around for a chair, "is all of you expect to find fullness in the same damn place . . . at the end of a gun or between a woman's legs."

"Where's Jesus?" Anthony asked, smiling broadly.

"Sleeping," Jane answered.